She felt the anger growing inside her like a dark cloud blocking out the sunlight. Her lips poked out with it, one hand closing in an impotent fist. It threatened to consume her as her fingers closed on the smooth object in her pocket. He didn't deserve her love. Maybe someone should teach him a lesson. Her eyes narrowed as he closed the distance between them and she came to a decision. She was just the woman to do it.

FALLING

NATALIE DUNBAR

Genesis Press Inc.

Indigo Love Stories

An imprint Genesis Press Publishing

Genesis Press, Inc.
P.O. Box 101
Columbus, MS 39703

ISBN 1-58571-121-7
Manufactured in the United States of America

Second Edition

Visit us at www.genesis-press.com
or call at 1-888-Indigo-1

ACKNOWLEDGEMENTS

Thanks to God for the will and the talent to put the stories in my head to paper in a way that provides enjoyment for others. Thanks to my immediate family for being patient, understanding, and supportive when I spent time writing and editing this manuscript and could have spent the time with them. Thanks to my sisters and brothers, "The Big Six," for their love and support. I want to thank my editor, Sidney Rickman, for shaping this manuscript and making it the best. Thanks to my critique group, Karen White Owens and Reon Laudat for critiques, input, suggestions, and great ideas. Thanks to all the readers who have written me, supported me, and continue to read my books. I really appreciate all of you.

Natalie Dunbar

PROLOGUE

The beautiful, famous, and wealthy had filled the candle-lit chapel and anxiously awaited the final moments. Imani Celeste, more beautiful than ever, graced the altar in an antique white Cara Sutton gown. A sheer veil streamed out from the silk and lace-accented gold circlet that adorned her long black hair. Her dark, exotic eyes sparkled, her lush lips smiled. At her side in a black tuxedo and antique white shirt with black accents, Perry Bonds, Detroit Pistons basketball star, gazed at his bride with love and adoration.

DeAndra sat midway back in the church, on the bride's side with Judge Damon Kessler. She stole a glance at the man who had loved and lost Imani. His fingers grasped the edge of the pew as if his life depended on it. Knowing that she could never stand to see Damon marry another woman, she understood how he felt. She loved Damon. Had loved him since she was a fifteen-year-old with everything but school on her mind. He'd been a young, very handsome and idealistic lawyer, who'd forced her to participate in her own defense in court for truancy and delinquency. He'd inspired her in the process. What a road they'd traveled.

Focusing on the happy couple, she leaned forward to hear them exchange their vows. It was done. They kissed passionately for several moments, then released each other to face the crowd.

When everyone stood to throw rice and blow bubbles as the couple started down the aisle, DeAndra heard Damon cough, and turned in time to see him swipe at his eyes with a thumb and forefinger.

She stared. Was he was actually crying? She couldn't tell for sure, but even the thought of him crying for Imani hurt her heart. She stiffened, a burning pain in her chest. Then she moved closer and slid her hand in his, silently reminding him that she was with him. When he didn't respond, she fought the sharp sting of rejection.

Outside the church, she stood in the line with him and watched him hug Imani, who told him how glad she was to see him. Damon wished her every happiness, then moved on to shake hands with Perry. When DeAndra extended a hand to Imani, she was enfolded in a hug. "Please take care of him," Imani whispered.

"If he lets me," DeAndra mumbled, aware that it was going to be hard.

"He does love you," Imani whispered back.

DeAndra moved on to congratulate Perry, suddenly aware of how hard it is to hate someone who nudges you towards what you want most and tells you what you want to hear.

Afterward, Damon was silent as he drove her home. Feeling a little low herself, DeAndra didn't push it.

"I'm not up to the reception, so I'm going to skip it," Damon told her as he stood at her front door.

"We could do something else," she suggested, not surprised when he declined, and throwing everything she had into being understanding.

"I just want to go home," he said.

DeAndra drew him into her arms and kissed him. "Take care of yourself."

When he hadn't so much as called two weeks later, DeAndra got her hair done, showered and donned a sexy red dress that clung to every perfumed curve. Then she assembled a care package of his favorite foods: 1993 Dom Perignon Champagne, succulent red strawberries dipped in gourmet chocolate, almonds and cashews, lobster tails and petite filet mignon, and Caesar salad. She knew she'd splurged, but Damon was worth it.

She stood on the porch a good ten minutes before he answered the bell. Usually impeccably dressed, Damon looked battered and depressed in a faded pair of navy blue sweats.

"Come in, DeAndra, we need to talk."

"I brought something for us to eat," she said brightly, letting him take the basket into the kitchen. She followed, noting the dusty tables, and the dirty dishes piled into the sink.

"I'm not very hungry." His eyes were flat and dull.

In the act of unloading the basket onto his kitchen counter, she stared at him, anger filling her up. Here he was wasting away because Imani hadn't had the good sense to realize that he was the better man. Not that she was sorry. She knew that she was the one he really needed, not Imani. If only he would give her a fourth of the love he'd lavished on the woman who was now Mrs. Perry Bonds. "Damon, she's married now."

His eyes turned towards her, stark and haunted. "Yes, I was there. I had to see it to believe it," he said in a harsh voice. "Now...now I need time to accept that and move on with my life."

DeAndra set the Dom Perignon on the counter, her heart pumping so hard that she struggled to catch her breath. "What are you trying to say?"

He motioned her to a seat beside him at the great room counter. "I'm trying to say that I've never made a secret of my feelings for Imani, and with everything that's happened, I've failed to clarify my feelings for you."

Beside him, her throat was dry as sawdust. She couldn't say a word.

Damon took her hand. "You're a lovely, intelligent, and very giving person, DeAndra, and I care for you very much. I'm not proud of the way I've behaved with you while I was going through my off again, on again engagement."

Standing, she sought to stop the flow of his words. "We *made love*, Damon."

He shook his head. "No. I used you and I'm ashamed. You deserve so much more."

Unadulterated pain seared her heart. Her eyelids stung as she fought tears. She was not going to cry. "Let me be the judge of what I deserve."

He grabbed her hand in frustration. "You don't understand. Things will never be the same. I've never felt so deeply and completely for anyone. I'm a mess. I don't have any more love to give, so you can't hang around hoping I'll grow to love you!"

DeAndra snatched her hand away and her voice rose in cutting fury. "You had to ruin everything, didn't you? I loved you. Do you hear me? I still love you and nothing's going to change that, but you don't have to worry about poor little DeAndra hanging around hoping you'll grow to love her. I'm done! I won't bother you again!"

Running to the other side of the counter, she grabbed her purse and jacket, and bolted from the house.

"DeAndra! DeAndra!" Damon called after her, his voice filled with regret.

She made it all the way to the car before a flood of tears blinded her. Feeling for the lock with shaking fingers, she fitted her key and locked the door. Inside, she blubbered like a baby and mopped vainly at the tears with a Kleenex.

Turning at the sight of movement, she saw that he was coming down the steps. Somehow she managed to start the car and drive away.

CHAPTER ONE

Two years later:

Judge Damon Kessler sat at the oak desk in his office making a last check of his travel itinerary and tickets. His secretary had already checked, but as a cautious man, he verified everything personally. Ascertaining that everything was in order, he made a quick check of the mail in his *In* box.

A white, personal-sized envelope addressed to him with the words *Private* scrolled across the center in black lettering caught his attention and triggered suspicion and alarm as he realized someone had slipped it into the mail. No stamp or return address. Drawing on a pair of vinyl gloves he'd bought for occasions like this, he slit the envelope with a letter opener and removed the folded paper. Smoothing the folds, he began to read the flowing script.

Darling,

Missed you at the park this morning. Are you avoiding me? I'm trying to understand, but your ignoring me is making me angry. Our love is too strong for us to let anyone or anything keep us apart. Come to me my love. Meet me at our special place and all will be forgiven.

Your one and only,

Jalanna

Damon reread the letter. With his last minute packing, he'd missed his morning run. Someone was obviously watching and keeping track of his movements and he didn't like it. He didn't know anyone named Jalanna. This was the third letter he'd received from this woman in six weeks. After receiving the first two, he discussed them with his friend Warfield Clay, who happened to be the chief of police for the city of

Detroit. Insisting he turn the letters over to the police, Clay had promised to look into it.

Like the other letters, this letter did not threaten harm, Damon decided as he dialed his friend, but he sensed escalating danger. He wasn't involved with anyone at the moment; in fact the thought hadn't even crossed his mind. It had taken time for him to get over his broken engagement to supermodel Imani Celeste nearly two years ago. He jealously guarded his heart these days.

The phone rang on the other end. Someone answered. "Clay here."

"Hey, this is Damon. What's up, brother?"

"We're still recovering from the blistering we got from the mayor and the newspapers on the drugs missing from the property room. We've got two investigations going on. I guarantee you this: Some heads are going to roll."

"Hmmmph!" Damon intoned sympathetically as he tilted his leather chair back and rocked. "Just make sure your head doesn't roll right along with theirs."

"Oh, I have no worries on that end," Clay replied confidently. "I'm just mad as hell that they had the balls to do it on my watch. I pride myself on running a tight ship. I've got plenty of controls in place that should have worked. We're going to get to the bottom of this, believe me." He paused. "So what's new on the legal front?"

"I'm headed down to D.C. for a legal summit on human rights in a couple of hours. I'm set to testify before ongress, along with a bunch of other legal eagles and then we're going to help draft some legislation and propose policy revisions," Damon replied.

Clay's voice rose. "I'm impressed. I heard about it on the news a few days ago, but I didn't release that it would be happening so soon."

"Yeah, well, time passes fast when you're having fun. Did your guys ever get anything on those letters I turned over?"

Clay's heavy sigh filled his ears. "Nothing conclusive. There were no fingerprints on them but yours. You're going to have to give the situation some time. If they start to threaten you, we'll get more proactive." His voice changed abruptly. "You didn't get another letter, did you?"

"Yeah, at the office this morning," Damon informed him as he looked down at graceful sailboats gliding down the Detroit River, eight stories below him. "There was still no real threat, but obviously this person is watching me. She knew that I didn't run this morning. She also sounds irritated that I haven't that I haven't been spending time with her…"

"Read it to me," Clay directed. "I want to get an idea of how serious this is."

Damon read it into the phone. When he finished, Clay asked, "You seeing anyone right now?"

"No. I've been calling on old friends for partners to attend social events. It's better that way."

Clay made a clicking sound with his teeth. "And you used to be something of a ladies man…"

Damon chuckled. "That's why I can give it all up without a qualm. I know exactly what I'm missing."

"Right now, it's probably a good thing that you're not seeing anyone. This situation seems to be escalating. Any woman you were seeing would be in danger, right along with you. In the way of advice, I can't tell you much, except to be careful and stick to your routine. Keep your eyes open for people who may be monitoring your activities. You got a gun?"

"You know I do," Damon reminded him, "ever since Marshall was acquitted and the victim's family threatened me and the jury."

"Just be careful," Clay reiterated. "Try not to shoot any innocent people, and put that letter in a courier envelope on your way out. I'll have it checked out."

Damon thanked him and slipped the letter into a courier envelope as soon as he got off the phone. Scrawling Clay's name and office address across the front, he took it to the outer office, along with the other mail for his secretary, Tori. She was seated at her desk talking with her friend Rachel, who worked somewhere in the building. No doubt they were setting up their weekend plans.

"Need me to do anything?" she asked brightly, straightening her shoulders in her new blue suit and trying to look professional as he entered.

"Just make sure this mail gets out," he answered pleasantly. "Hello, Rachel. How's life treating you?"

As usual, color rushed into her light brown face and her eyes held a strange intensity that sometimes threw him. From his secretary, he knew that she was painfully shy and in counseling somewhere. She stammered her answer. "I-I'm fine, Judge Kessler. And you?"

"I'm not complaining." He smiled reassuringly. "Besides, who would listen?"

"I would," Tori piped up with a swing of her dark brown ponytail. "Isn't that what you pay me to do?"

"No, that's not in your job description," he assured her, "but some people might file it under other duties as assigned. I don't expect you to do anything other than perform your job to the best of your ability."

"Okay, boss," Tori laughed, "I'm here for complaint duty, if you need me."

"Me too," Rachel added.

"Noted and appreciated, ladies." Damon glanced at his watch. "I'd better get out of here."

"W-Will you be back soon?" Rachel asked, surprising both Damon and Tori.

Damon scanned her, taking in her innocent expression. He didn't like giving out details of his trips unless it was work or safety related. Then he reminded himself that Rachel was harmless. "Yes," he said, breaking the awkward silence, "I'll just be gone two or three days."

"Have a safe trip!" both girls called as he stepped back into his office to retrieve his coat and briefcase.

"Where's he going?" he heard Rachel ask. Tori launched into an explanation of his trip to Washington as he hustled out.

In an office on the south side of Chicago, DeAndra Blake checked her paperwork and made a few notes on her legal pad. The combined light from the stark light bulb in the ceiling and from the large lamp she'd brought from home was not enough. She glanced at the old clock that graced the wall of the legal aid center and slanted a glance at the little girl standing on a step stool as she busily filed papers. "Mouse, it's nearly seven-thirty. Shouldn't you be leaving? I don't want your Mama worrying about you."

"It's okay," the little girl squeaked in her high-pitched voice. "Mama's not home. She had an appointment with the doctor."

"Are you sure?" DeAndra peeked out the cheap white blinds and saw that the sun had dropped and the light was fading. It took longer for darkness to fall now that spring had arrived.

"I'm sure," Mouse said with confidence, her two long, thick, black braids bobbing. "You can call the house. Nobody's there."

Setting her notes aside, DeAndra decided to do just that. She knew all about little girls who had better things to do than go to school or home. She'd been one of them. Thank God, she'd been lucky. No one had harmed her, but she'd gotten into some dangerous scrapes.

Hopefully Mouse would do better. With a mother who worked two jobs and a family more often missing than not, she sometimes worried about Mouse. That's why DeAndra had gotten the mother's permission and put the girl to work when she began hanging out at the center on Saturdays.

Lifting the receiver on the phone, she dialed Mouse's home. The phone rang six times before she gave up.

"Told you," Mouse said in a self-important tone. Her two front teeth stuck out prominently in her milk-chocolate colored face, giving her an impish smile.

DeAndra raised an eyebrow and gave her the eye.

"I wasn't getting smart!" Mouse said defensively.

"I didn't say you were," DeAndra said calmly. "I just want you to watch your mouth when you're talking to grown-ups."

"Yes ma'am."

DeAndra decided to let that one pass. Mouse was simply not a yes ma'am sort of girl. "I'll drop you off on my way home," DeAndra told her. "It's getting too late for you to be out there by yourself."

"Okay," the little girl said. "Got some more work for me to do?"

"Yes. You can sharpen the pencils and empty the waste basket into that bin at the end of the hall while I finish up."

When the child moved to obey, DeAndra went back to scribbling notes on her pad. Most of the cases at the center revolved around disputes with landlords, but a few also involved assault, child abuse, and petty crimes. Working at the center on Saturdays was her way of giving back to the community in much the same way that she'd been helped. She would have preferred to do it in Detroit, but she'd moved to Chicago two years earlier. The community had welcomed her.

Finishing her notes, DeAndra stood and put everything away. Mouse was sitting at the other old wooden desk, quietly drawing. *She's basically a good child*, DeAndra thought as she stepped across the green and white tiles and removed her coat from the hanger on the back of the door. While she retrieved her purse from a locked drawer, Mouse stood, folding her drawing.

"May I see?" DeAndra asked.

The little girl unfolded the sheet to reveal a pretty young woman with eyes that were much older than she looked. A bone-deep weariness filled the woman's expression and dulled her smile. "It's my mama!" Mouse explained.

"Yes, I recognize your mother," DeAndra said, still examining the penciled drawing. "You did a good job. Maybe you're going to be an artist when you grow up."

Mouse smiled and thanked her for the compliment. "I'm going to be a lawyer just like you when I grow up."

"I'm flattered," DeAndra said, shrugging into her black jacket. "If you still want to be a lawyer when you grow up, you can do it."

"Then, I could go to Washington to testify before Congress, too?" Mouse asked.

"Sure, if that's what you want to do," DeAndra assured her.

Mouse refolded the paper and got her coat. Then they got the security guard at the front desk to walk them to the car.

Not certain there would be food for Mouse at home, DeAndra stopped by Mickey Dee's and bought a children's meal for Mouse and grilled chicken and a side salad for herself. When she pulled up in front of the house, the lights were on and a raggedy old blue Ford was parked in the driveway.

Mouse fell silent, her eyes unusually large.

Getting out of the car, DeAndra walked around to the passenger side. Mouse was already standing on the grass. "Looks like your mother's home," she remarked, giving the child her bag of food.

"That's not Mama, that's Uncle Eric." Her mouth formed a straight line.

DeAndra attributed the loss of natural exuberance in the child's voice to a reluctance to be home. She used to feel that way herself. "Okay." She lifted the soft drink from the caddy between the seats and gave it to the child. "Do you have your key?" she asked, slamming the car door shut.

Mouse raised the hand with the soft drink to show the blue plastic coil bracelet with the key dangling from it, and they headed for the porch. The front door opened just as they reached the top step. DeAndra stared at the man who answered, trying to keep her expression neutral.

The man's bald head reflected the light as he stood in the doorway in loose jeans and a white T-shirt decorated with the picture of a rap group, but his feral eyes demanded her attention. He looked as if he could kill as easily as look at someone and he reeked of alcohol. Uncle or not, DeAndra wouldn't have left her child with him.

"Uncle Eric, this is Ms. Blake. Mama…"

He focused on Mouse. "Where you been?" he interrupted. "You know you was 'sposed to get home before dark."

Concerned for Mouse, DeAndra spoke. "She's been at the neighborhood legal services center with me. The time got away from us. I called, but…"

"I was talking to Michelle," he broke in rudely, using Mouse's proper name. "I want to hear what she got to say."

As Mouse launched into a hasty explanation, his eyes narrowed. "Get in here!" he spat.

The child scrambled through the door, holding tightly to her food.

Standing on the porch, DeAndra wanted to snatch the child and run with her, but years of training kept her in check. She had no legal standing as far as Mouse was concerned. Mouse's uncle had obviously taken an instant dislike to DeAndra.

Tilting his head, he stretched his eyes, mocking her. Then he extended a finger and shut the door in her face.

DeAndra blinked. *The nerve of that man!* She let loose a string of curses under her breath as she turned and took the steps. She liked Mouse's mother, but her brother was another story. Hopefully Mouse wouldn't get a spanking.

Determinedly releasing her doubts about the entire situation, she got into her car and forced her thoughts to the trip ahead. The firm had already purchased her tickets and made hotel reservations. Tonight she planned to fine-tune her testimony.

CHAPTER TWO

Washington, D.C.

Members of congress and their staff trekked the echoing white halls to fill the congressional chamber, their numbers buoyed by attorneys and judges who had come to testify before Congress. An air of expectancy and importance permeated the air and spurred each of the Human Rights Summit participants on as lawyers and judges prepared to testify.

The movement of people in and out of the chamber and through the halls formed an intricate pattern that Damon hoped would get them closer to their goal of impacting the nation's policies and laws on human rights. In his favorite blue pin-stripped Armani suit, Damon stood in the hallway outside the chamber, where reporters were interviewing a number of people. Several broadcast journalists had requested interviews with Damon.

"Judge Kessler, how did you become involved in the human rights movement?" a dark-haired, middle-aged reporter from ABC News asked, sticking a microphone in Damon's face.

"I love this country and I love the law," Damon began. "I've always wanted to devote my skills and talents to helping to resolve the compelling issues confronting this country relative to the rights of its citizens. My family has a rich history of involvement in human and civil rights movements. As you know, my grandfather, retired Judge Creighton Kessler, was an important part of the civil rights movement in the sixties. My father, Judge Darryl Kessler, continued the tradition until his death."

The ABC news reporter fired another question. "How did that

translate into your role in the summit this week?"

Damon gave him the same answer he'd given the reporters in Detroit. "When the organizers of this summit approached me, I was excited at the prospect and glad to lend my efforts to the task. I even managed to bring a few colleagues on board."

A female reporter from CNN stepped forward with her mike. "Could you give us some details on the myriad issues under the Human Rights Summit umbrella?"

Damon nodded. "Certainly. Human rights are concerned with the erosion of rights and liberties in America, especially in the face of gross terrorist activities. Human rights encompass women's rights in the United States, Europe, and around the world, racism in any form, and discrimination on the basis of disability, sex, color, or national origin. The death penalty, educational and employment opportunities for everyone, and voting rights are also very important issues that fall under the Human Rights Summit Umbrella."

"Several of the issues you've mentioned are also considered civil rights issues," the CNN reporter noted.

Damon smiled. "Civil rights and human rights are interrelated. At the heart of the civil rights movement is belief in the basic human dignity of all people and their right to live in freedom with justice and equal opportunity."

Tom Renshaw, a noted national news heavyweight anchor, flashed a smile full of charm. "I enjoyed your testimony, Judge Kessler, as I'm sure everyone in the chambers did, but what specifically are you hoping to accomplish in Washington this week with this Human Rights Summit?"

Damon paused and looked straight into the camera. "We have several issues to address here in Washington this week. Along with my fellow judges and other members of the legal profession, we hope to call attention to the sorry state of human rights in today's world and persuade Congress and the president to do more to alleviate the situation at home and abroad. Some of the present policies mock the spirit of our Constitution and the soul of our nation."

Tom Renshaw nodded approvingly. "You've mentioned some of the policies in question several times, sir. Finally, how will you measure the success of this summit?"

Damon nodded, his gaze level. "This summit has already earned a significant measure of success in my opinion by calling attention to the human rights issues facing us as a nation. If some of our initiatives or the language and legislation drafted this week make their way into the laws of our nation, our success will be overwhelming."

Satisfied with the interview, Damon waited for Renshaw to close. The interview had been all he'd hoped for.

The national news anchor beamed and shook Damon's hand enthusiastically. "Thank you, sir. Good luck this week." As Damon returned his thanks and stepped aside, Renshaw faced the camera. "You've been listening to U.S. District Court Judge Damon Kessler, from the eastern district of Michigan, which includes the 34 counties which form the eastern half of Michigan's lower peninsula. He's here in Washington this week for the Human Rights Summit. This is Tom Renshaw, reporting live from Washington for CBS News' *National News that Affects You.*

"Good interview," Damon's associate and former law clerk, Myron, murmured as they stepped back into the chamber. "I've heard some great testimony today, yours among the best of it."

Damon thanked him. "When are you scheduled to testify?" he asked, preparing to place his notes back into his leather briefcase. Balancing it against his midsection, he carefully flipped the metal locks and prepared to slip the notes in.

Myron checked his watch. "I've got about an hour."

"Well, I'm anxious to hear what you have to say." The briefcase shifted suddenly and the bundle of notes slipped from Damon's grasp and fluttered to the floor. The crowd around them parted as he bent down to pick them up. At his left, Myron captured some of the way-ward paper.

Damon was gathering the last sheet when the confident click of a pair of high heels sounded above the noise of the crowd, commanding his attention. He turned to look, then stared. It had been a long time since he'd stopped to experience and appreciate the physical beauty of a woman.

Even from several feet away, the view from just above the polished tile floor was exciting. As inconspicuously as possibly, in as conservative a manner as possible, he looked first at a provocative pair of red and black high heels showcasing dainty feet, then followed the shapely brown legs of the petite wearer past exquisite knees to a hint of the sexy curve of thigh. The short, red skirt of the power suit teased and hinted at the treasures beneath. That walk intrigued him. Those legs fascinated him. Then the realization hit him. He recognized those legs. *DeAndra!*

Shock reverberated through him as he rose quickly with the papers in his hand. He felt as if he'd been punched in the midsection. Looking around, he saw that she'd already disappeared into the crowd.

"Mmmmph! Did you see that?" Myron remarked, "Now that's someone I'd like to know better!"

"DeAndra!" Damon stepped into the crowd, calling her name. The urge to speak to her overwhelmed him. Was he imagining the vulnerable note in his voice? Some people turned at the sound of his voice, but there was no sign of DeAndra.

"You know her?" Myron asked incredulously.

"She used to be one of my law clerks," Damon said, leaving out more than he could ever hope to explain. "She was one of the best." He wondered if she'd heard him call her name. Most of all he wondered if she could ever forgive him for the selfish way he'd treated her. He'd used DeAndra to salve his ego and hurt her terribly in the process. When he'd come out of his deep funk, she'd already disappeared.

Myron stared silently at Damon, eyes full of questions he had the sense to leave unasked.

Turning away from him, Damon caught sight of DeAndra at the stand below the podium. She'd always been pretty in a delicate sort of way. Now she'd blossomed into a beautiful woman. Her hair was still short, but her current style with curling strands flipped up and framing her face reminded him of the style that actress Halle Berry favored. Exquisite makeup emphasized her golden brown eyes and the lush fullness of her bottom lip.

Damon struggled to keep his thoughts in the present. They'd shared so many memories, from the time she'd been a promising child till the time she'd been one of his best clerks, working for his friends. He'd even been there when her beloved grandmother died. The connection was still there. Damon wanted to be in her company, to talk to her and see her smile. She had a warm heart and a beautiful smile that had never failed to tug at his heartstrings. How could he have messed things up so badly?

Stepping quickly through the maze of people in order to arrive at the podium on time, DeAndra started and turned. She'd heard someone in the crowd calling her name. Scanning the people laughing, talking, gesturing, and generally filling the time until the next person testified, she didn't recognize anyone.

Continuing on past the seated members of Congress, she took her place at the newly vacated stand behind the podium. As her predecessor began to speak, the crowd quieted. DeAndra studied her notes and silently rehearsed her speech. She'd already checked her hair, makeup, and clothing.

Her predecessor finished his testimony and was thanked by the Speaker of the House. Given the signal, she listened as she was introduced and thanked the speaker. Stepping onto the podium, she took a deep breath, and began to speak calmly. The audience's attention reached out to her like a void just waiting to be filled. She made eye contact with as many people as possible, though she remembered to also gaze directly into the cameras.

Testifying before Congress was an honor she wouldn't soon forget, and an opportunity to expand her horizons and her network of influential people. She knew that her mother, her brother, and the partners and associates at Hartfield, Merrien, and Sawyer, were watching. Suddenly her gaze connected with a familiar pair of sea green eyes and her words faltered. *Damon Kessler!*

Behind the podium her knees wobbled, threatening her delicate balance on the three-inch heels. She gripped the podium with icy hands. Already pounding with all the excitement, her heart somehow accelerated. Her throat threatened to close as beads of sweat broke out on her nose. Swallowing painfully, she nevertheless continued smoothly, her gaze firmly on the members of Congress. The temporary lapse had been so small that most people hadn't noticed.

As she finished, the Speaker of the House thanked her for her eloquent testimony and DeAndra responded politely. Leaving the podium, she disappeared into the crowd, maneuvered around various ongoing interviews with television reporters, and made a beeline for the exit.

"You did good, DeAndra," an associate said as she walked by. "But I thought you were going to stay to hear the rest of the testimony."

"I—I'm not feeling so well," she replied. "I'm going back to the hotel. I'll probably see you later."

"Feel better. We'll call you later." The words spurred DeAndra on.

You're acting like a coward, the voice at the back of her thoughts accused. She didn't care. Those green eyes had brightened when she met his gaze. Their next meeting would be up close and personal. She wasn't ready to face Damon. Didn't need his intrusion into her life. Even after two years, she'd only had to see his face for all the feelings she'd been holding in check to spill out to torment her. It made her want to cry all over again. DeAndra's lips tightened. *Get your shit together, girl!*

Outside the chamber, she forced air into her lungs and relaxed her fists. She reminded herself that she knew the man almost as well as she knew herself. The only way she'd get through this was to show no sign of weakness. It was the only way to convince Damon to stay out of her life.

Exiting the building, DeAndra caught a cab back to her hotel. Sitting in the back, all the feelings of pain, uncertainty, love and rejection washed over her. She shivered with a trembling weakness that shook her to her very core.

He'd never lied to her, and told her that he loved her, but she'd been certain she could make things work between them because she'd had enough love for both of them. Now she knew that Damon Kessler was a one-woman man and Imani Celeste Bonds was the only woman he would ever love. DeAndra had done her best to give up her dream of a life with Damon. She'd already shed too many tears for him.

As the cab drove past the Smithsonian, she straightened in the seat. The next time she saw Damon Kessler, she'd be ready for him.

Back in her luxurious hotel room, DeAndra watched the rest of the Human Rights Summit testimony on television. She started when the phone rang and took her time answering. Her tone was controlled when she spoke into the receiver.

"Dee? I almost gave up on you being there! Whatcha doing, girl?" Her brother Larry's booming voice filled her ear.

A wave of warmth coursed through her. "I was just relaxing and watching the rest of the testimony and interviews."

"Hey, we saw your testimony on television. I'm proud of you, sis, and I got it all on tape! You can watch it over and over again, the way Mama's been doing. We're even going to send a copy to Mack in Germany."

Thanking him, DeAndra chuckled as her mother got on the phone.

"Aw hush up, boy, you're just jealous!" Her mother teased gruffly. "DeAndra, you've done your Mama proud. I got tears in my eyes just listening to you speak. You just keep on getting better. I know that you're going places you haven't even dreamed of. I want the world to know how proud I am of my girl."

DeAndra's heart swelled with pride and she blinked back tears. It wasn't often that she earned her mother's praise. "Thank you, Mama.

Larry's voiced boomed into the receiver once more and she could almost see his animated face and sharp brown eyes. "Dee, I saw that judge you used to hang with on television too. Did you see him? Are you two kickin' it like old times?"

"I only saw him for a minute in a crowd," she answered. "I wasn't looking for him."

"Well, he's probably looking for you. You were so down when you left Detroit that I never told you how hard he tried to get your new address and phone number. You never said a word, but I figured that he must have hurt you some kind of way, so I blew him off."

"You did the right thing," DeAndra told him in a tone that only fluctuated a little.

"Just what did he do?" Larry persisted.

DeAndra sighed. "Since you've waited this long to ask, let's just leave it. I've grown up a lot since then."

"You sure?"

"Yes, I'm sure," she answered firmly.

"I know you used to be crazy about him," Larry continued, pushing the issue.

Pursing her lips, she told a bold-faced lie. "It was just a crush, you know, puppy love."

Larry apparently knew better. "Yeah, but I didn't know puppy love could last so long."

DeAndra made a clicking sound with her teeth. "You're treading on thin ice, brother. There's a lot I could ask you, such as what ever happened to that girlfriend who looked like she could bench press you and a couple of your friends? I bet Mama would like to hear the answer to that one too."

Larry cackled with laughter on the other end of the phone. "So, when are you going back to Chicago?"

DeAndra smiled. "Better, much better. I'll be back by Sunday afternoon. Are you planning to visit?"

"Yeah, as soon as this semester is over. Otherwise, I would have to come on a Friday and go back on Saturday so I can do my homework."

"I'd love to have you," she said sincerely. "I can't wait to show you my new place."

Afterward, she lay across her bed with her eyes closed. Later she met a few of her associates for a seafood buffet dinner at Philips Flagship, on the waterfront.

The next day DeAndra spent the morning working with a group of lawyers and Congressional staffers. She'd been assigned to the group working on recommendations for U.S. policy in dealing with foreign countries. Several ideas were aired and considered. Then, just before lunch, they divided the list into sections for each member of the group to work on. Agreeing to meet back with everyone at two o'clock, DeAndra went to lunch.

Walking the busy streets near the building, she wound up in a little gourmet delicatessen on Pennsylvania Avenue. It was crowded, but the aromatic scents of corned beef, pastrami, and dill pickles wafting through the air combined to make her mouth water and her stomach whine. She waited five minutes, but she finally got a little wooden table in a corner. Then she placed her order and settled down with her notes while she waited.

Going through her section of recommendations one by one, she tuned out the ambient noise of people talking, eating, ordering, and preparing food. With a red pen, she marked sentences, occasionally pausing to chew thoughtfully on the end. From time to time she sipped her bottled water.

A man's voice elevated itself above the background noise, breaking her concentration. "Excuse me, do you mind if I sit here?"

Knowing the place was crowded, DeAndra answered automatically. "No, of course not." She glanced up from her notes to see Damon Kessler standing at her table. Her fingers gripped the pin so hard that it bit into her hand. Smothering a curse under her breath, she wondered how he'd managed to find her. He'd been nowhere in sight when she'd ducked out of the Congressional committee building. "Damon." She gulped down water, her throat impossibly tight and dry.

"It's been a long time," he said in that deep, sensual voice. His green eyes sparkled, but there were hints of uncertainty in their depths.

"Yes, it has." She recovered. "You're looking well." He'd aged a little, she thought, noting the fine lines around his eyes and the fact that he'd lost weight. DeAndra knew that depression and loss could do that to a person. Despite the lines, he looked handsome and distinguished in his custom-made gray suit and silk tie. DeAndra could see that she wasn't the only woman in the delicatessen who'd noticed either. He was a man who would always draw the avid attention of the opposite sex without any effort on his part.

Despite the strong, provocative scents of corned beef, pastrami, salami, and ham wafting through the air, she inhaled the closer, familiar scent of Damon and his cologne. She forced it out on a sigh, but the sensual memories it evoked remained. "We're going to have to catch up sometime. Right now, I've got work to do before we meet back at two."

"I understand completely. I just finished some committee work myself." He drew out the chair across from her and sat in it. "I'm happy to just sit here, watch you work, and reflect on how much you've matured."

Narrowing her eyes, DeAndra bit back a nasty comment and bent back to her work. This was her table. He wasn't going to spoil her lunch. Unfortunately, his very closeness made it hard for her to work. She found herself reading each sentence over and over. Her body vibrated with excitement and her brain shut down. She underlined and made marks with her pen anyway.

A waitress bustled over and took Damon's order. Shortly after that, DeAndra's lunch arrived. The corned beef sandwich on rye was humongous. Thick slices of Swiss cheese protruded from the sides. In addition, she'd ordered potato salad and dill pickles. She realized that she was going to have trouble eating just half the food.

"Would you like to split your food?" Damon asked, correctly sizing the situation up. "I'd be happy to pay for everything."

"That's not necessary," she told him. "I make more than enough to pay for lunch." She could remember when he had always been the one to pay, whether it was her lunch, or sweets she craved, or even a few things she needed that her family couldn't afford.

Inclining his head in agreement, he called the waitress, cancelled his food order, and obtained another plate.

Dividing the food, she stifled the urge to apologize for acting like a spoiled brat. Damon knew as well as she did what the real problem was. He'd hurt her badly and she wasn't about to forgive or forget. The very fact that he was sitting with her now indicated that he was going to press the issue. He'd been more than just a mentor and a lover; he'd been her friend.

DeAndra squirted mustard on her half of the sandwich and bit into it. The combined flavor of hot corned beef, Swiss cheese, and rye bread was so good that she momentarily forgot about him. She savored each bite and scooped up spoonfuls of mustard potato salad in between.

"You've grown into a very beautiful woman and from what I hear, a hell of a lawyer," he murmured.

Glancing at him, she thanked him for the compliments. Then she sat munching the dill pickles.

Damon bit into his half of the sandwich, chewed, and swallowed. "Your testimony before Congress yesterday was accurate and moving."

"You really think so?" The question was out before she realized it. No matter how she felt about him personally, she still valued Damon Kessler's opinion.

"Yes, I do," he answered in a serious tone. "I hope your family recorded it."

"They did. I missed your testimony, but I've heard it was excellent," she said.

Damon responded politely. They finished their lunch in relative silence.

As she gathered her papers to hurry back to her meeting, he made his move. "Could we meet for dinner tonight? There's a lot I need to say…"

"No. It's not necessary, Damon. What happened is in the past and I-I want to keep it there." DeAndra stood and slung her purse over her shoulder. She lifted the stack of papers.

Fixing her with his gaze, Damon's voice rang with a sincerity that demanded her attention. "Please, DeAndra, words cannot express how much I regret…"

That vulnerable feeling that she hated overwhelmed her. DeAndra clenched her fingers around the strap of her purse. "I said no, Damon, and I meant it." She pitched her voice low, but her words and tone left no doubts.

Ignoring the sudden attention of the other diners, DeAndra turned and walked away from him as fast as she could in her heels. When she made it out into the sunshine and fresh air, she felt better.

Walking back to the building among the amiable people filling the sidewalks, she worked on her section of the recommendations in her thoughts.

Damon sat at the table and finished his lunch. He'd followed DeAndra to the deli in hope of clearing the air and settling things between them. From the stubborn jut of her chin to the cold politeness in her golden brown eyes, he'd known he'd have a battle on his hands. DeAndra was a fiery and passionate woman. Her cool, polite manner was simply an act. The hurt he'd felt when she made her hasty exit cut deep because she was someone he really cared about.

He felt a connection to her that he knew would never go away. He didn't know what he'd been thinking when he'd fallen into bed with her. Shaking his head, he amended the thought with the obvious. He'd been thinking with the head that didn't have a brain.

When he'd come out of his deep funk from losing Imani, he'd tried to find her, but had eventually given up. Her family had been angry with him and refused to give him any information. He'd thrown himself into his work and his love of the law. That's what made his life worth living.

Pushing back his chair, Damon stood. He wasn't ready to give up on DeAndra just yet. He simply needed to change his strategy.

CHAPTER THREE

It was nearly five o'clock when DeAndra left the Congressional committee building. She rubbed her dry eyes and blinked, rolling her shoulders. Working with the Congressional staffers had been every bit as draining as working her caseload in Chicago, but she loved the idea of making a difference in her world. What she was doing was important. It gave her hope for the future. In an effort to reward herself for the long day, she strolled to the Metro station in the warm spring air.

All around her cherry blossoms waved in the light breeze and signs pointed the way to many of D.C.'s famous landmarks. Simply reading the names filled her with anticipation and excitement. Tomorrow, only half a day of committee work was scheduled and the following day, none, so that all of the Human Rights Summit participants could tour the city. She'd already read the itinerary and was looking forward to visiting the White House, the Lincoln and Washington Memorials, the Smithsonian, and the Tomb of the Unknown Soldier.

Standing at the metro train stop, she closed her eyes against the still bright sunshine and breathed in the rich fragrance of flowers. She yawned. Despite the excitement of Washington, she was tired. The prospect of sampling the nightlife with some of the other attorneys suddenly seemed less appealing. Though there had been periods in her life when good times and partying had absorbed a lot of her time, hard work now consumed most of her waking hours. She bargained with herself. Maybe if she had a nap…

When the train came, she boarded and stood like several other the passengers, in the aisle holding on to the rails as it took off. With interest, she eyed the crowd of professional people. The women wore fashionable suits and career-wear, and several of the men wore designer suits. Both men and women carried briefcases. The tourists stood out because of their maps and avid attention to the route diagrams.

Exiting at her station, DeAndra took the escalator up to the next level and walked to her hotel. As she strolled through the lobby, the bell captain greeted her, a hint of amused excitement behind his smile. She returned the greeting, a little puzzled, then continued on to her room.

DeAndra slipped the card into the slot and pulled it out. When she opened the door, the heady scent of flowers greeted her. The room was filled with a riot of flowers. She stepped into her room and gaped. The room was filled with flowers: red, pink, and white chrysanthemums to yellow tulips and purple iris, plush red roses, fragrant white lilies, frangipani, orchids, and bird of paradise. The roomed smelled like a flower garden. Every type of vase imaginable, from fancy crystal and thin white columns, to delicate flowered teapots, covered every available surface, including the plush floral sofa and matching recliner.

Closing and locking the door, DeAndra leaned against it and surveyed the room. The effect of the exotic array of flowers was overwhelming. It was the type of extravagant gesture she'd read about, but never experienced. She didn't need to look at the cards attached to each arrangement to know that Damon Kessler had sent the flowers. He'd obviously gone to a lot of trouble and expense. Although she felt that the gesture was touching, at the same time it made her feel crowded.

Dropping her briefcase by the coffee table, she kicked off her shoes and leaned over to roll the thigh high stockings down and off. She couldn't help wondering what he really wanted. Her jaw tightened. As she threaded her way through the pots and vases lining the floor, she decided that whatever it was, he wasn't going to get it.

Her bedroom was blessedly free of flowers except for the gorgeous basket of red, white, and yellow roses resting in the center of her bed. With a finger, she traced the petal soft edges of a yellow rose, and then leaned close to catch a whiff of its fresh scent. Closing her eyes, she brushed it against her cheek. As she lifted the basket and placed it on the nightstand, sentimental emotion welled up to stick in her throat.

Against her better judgment, she plucked the folded card from the basket and opened it. Damon's confident scrawl stood out in blue ink against the embossed linen cream:

DeAndra,

Words cannot express…

Please accept these flowers as tokens of my sincere regret.

Good friends make life worth living.

Damon

Clearing her throat on a sigh, she dropped the card on the table. She wished she could forget about him, but she couldn't. The two things she'd learned about herself when they'd been apart were that she was a one-man woman, and the type of woman who loved hard. Damon would always be the man she loved, whether she acted on it or not.

Her eyelids stung, but she pushed past thoughts of Damon. Blinking quickly, she checked the clock. There was still time to nap and get something to eat before hitting the clubs with the group.

She removed her short pink and green-checked jacket and placed it on a hanger. Her fingers were fumbling with the button on her skirt when a knock sounded on the door. Threading her way through the flowers, she made it to the door and checked through the peephole. A beefy black man in a bright blue cape stood outside the door. He was clean-shaven and his black hair was neatly trimmed. His smile was friendly and confident.

"Yes?" she called in an authoritative voice, thinking someone had the wrong room.

"Telegram for Ms. DeAndra Blake." He brandished an employee ID card.

She'd never received a telegram before. Had something happened to her mother or her brothers? The choked feeling in her throat resurfaced. She opened the door with the chain on to look at his card. "I'll take it."

The man smiled. "Miss Blake, this is a singing telegram. I can perform in the hall if you'd like, but you have to be able to see and hear everything."

"Oh." Relief coursed through her. DeAndra lifted the chain and opened the door, her curiosity getting the better of her. "I guess you can do it in the kitchen."

Following her back to the suite's kitchen, he dropped the edges of his cape to reveal a bright blue Superman costume with a red 'S' emblazed across his muscular chest. That startled her. It took a lot of nerve for a man his size to go around in a Superman costume. In the kitchen, he positioned himself in the center of the floor. She stood in the doorway to watch.

"This telegram is from Mr. Damon Kessler," he announced and then he began to sing an adaptation of the Anita Baker tune, "I Apologize" in a deep, moving baritone.

"I apologize, DeAndra, I do. My apology is real, honest, and true." He got down on one knee and spread his arms. "Yes, I know I know I was wrong, that's why I'm singing this song and I want to get through to you… I apologize, for I've been unkind, and I wish that I…"

When the song was done, she clapped enthusiastically and drew some money from the pocket of her skirt.

Standing, the man shook his head. "Thanks, but Mr. Kessler paid for everything." He gave her a card. "He's at this number waiting for your call."

DeAndra thanked him and let him out. Then she stared at the card, not sure what she was going to do. She'd enjoyed the performance, and was touched by Damon's thoughtfulness, but she knew that spending time with him would only make things worse for her. Still, she guessed that Damon wasn't going to give up until she relented and accepted his apology. *That's it! I'll just accept his apology and let that be the end of it.*

In another hotel a few blocks away, Damon stood at the closet selecting something to wear to dinner with some of his old college buddies who were now a part of the D.C. political scene. After wearing suits all week, he wanted to wear something casual. It was a shame that he'd never fully replaced his wardrobe after he'd lost so much weight. Most of his casual clothing was too big and definitely out of style.

He glanced at the clock across the room. It was 6:15. Then he checked the phone, willing it to ring. DeAndra should have received the telegram he'd sent. Although he had doubts regarding her response, he looked forward to her call. Reasoning with himself, he decided that if she did call, it wouldn't be right away. She could be very stubborn when the mood struck her.

Palming his room key, Damon left the room and headed for one of the men's shops he'd seen in the lobby. As he stepped into the elevator, he saw Colton Roberts, one of his classmates from his days at the University of Detroit. He got back off to greet him.

The two men clasped hands in the brothers' handshake and hugged briefly, patting each other on the back. "Man, I was hoping I'd run into you," Colton said. "It's been a long time. What have you been up to?"

"Just keeping busy with my cases, mentoring my clerks, and helping with the curriculum and law review program at the University of Detroit," Damon replied. "What about you?"

"I quit Stout, Blake, and Peterson and started my own firm in Ohio. I also got married a couple of months ago."

"Congratulations! How is it working out for you?" Damon asked as they both got on the empty, mirrored elevator.

Colton grinned. "The practice? Great! The marriage? Even better!" He patted his thick waistline. "Marriage agrees with me, man."

Maybe a little too much, Damon thought, chuckling.

"How about you? I don't want to rub it in, but there was no way anyone could miss the wedding of the century with all that press. Miss Imani got away from you, but I don't think she was the one. Have you found a good replacement yet?"

Damon met his gaze head-on. "No, man, and I'm not looking. I'm doing fine on my own. When I want companionship, I've got it. I've never had a problem."

As the elevator doors opened on the hotel lobby, Colton held up one hand in a gesture of acknowledgement. "Okay, man. I'm reading you loud and clear. If you should change your mind, my wife, Tiffany, has some unattached friends she's trying to hook up. They've got a lot going for them, they're all nice ladies, and some are real attractive."

They stepped off the elevator and stood at the side for a moment.

"That would be difficult, with you living in Ohio," Damon remarked.

"Not really." Colton pulled a card from a pocket and gave it to Damon. "Tiffany's closest friends are her sorority sisters and they're all over. Think about it, okay?"

Damon nodded. "Sure. Are you meeting with the group for dinner and drinks later?"

"I'll see you guys for drinks, but I promised Tiffany dinner on the waterfront. I'm going to have to introduce you two before we go back to Ohio."

"Okay, then I'll look forward to it, and I'll see you a little later on." At Colton's nod, Damon turned and made his way into the lobby shop just down the way.

The clothing in the lobby shop was as expensive as Damon had expected, but he was glad of the selection. Going through the piles of sweaters and slacks, he selected a designer silk sweater and coordinating slacks in chocolate and cream, and another set in a blue-green motif that the saleswoman claimed emphasized his green eyes.

When Damon got back to his room, the phone was ringing. Closing the door and placing his packages on the coffee table, he lifted the receiver and spoke. "This is Damon Kessler."

"Damon, this is DeAndra."

"It's so good to hear your voice. I'm glad you called," he said, savoring the sweet but feisty sound of her voice.

"Well, I really called to thank you for the flowers," she said a bit defensively. "They were beautiful. I got the singing telegram too. That was thoughtful of you. Thank you, Damon."

"You're welcome. Does this mean you're accepting my apology?"

"Uh, I guess so."

"Aren't you certain?" he asked, a little amused by her words and her tone.

"Yes."

"I just wanted to sure that there was no anger—"

"I got over that a long time ago."

"Or pain lingering on," he finished.

For several moments, she was silent. "I was almost over it, Damon. Why didn't you just leave me alone?"

"Because I care about you. I would have pressed the issue sooner if I'd been able to find you."

"Then care enough to give me more time and space."

"I don't think that's what you need."

"I do, and it's what I want."

He lifted the pen on the nightstand and began to doodle on the hotel pad. "DeAndra, you just accepted my apology. When I accept an apology, it means I'll do my best to forgive and forget what happened."

"As you said, that's what you do. I'm working on the 'forgive' part Damon. That's why I need time and space. As for forgetting, I don't think I can and I don't think I should. I learned a valuable lesson."

"What lesson did you learn?" he asked softly.

"I learned that I had you on a mile high pedestal and that I helped you fall off of it. You were my hero, Damon. My world revolved around you. I idolized you."

"I didn't need you to idolize me! Whatever girlish notions you may have projected on to me, I was and am what I've always been, a man. I'm only human, DeAndra. No matter how hard I try, I still make mistakes."

"I loved you, Damon. That's why I did everything I could to get your attention. But your heart was never big enough to include me and it never will be. You gave your heart to Imani."

Damon's voice shook with emotion. "I will never apologize for loving Imani or anyone else, because love is where you find it. DeAndra, it's a gift, whether it's returned or not. You're wrong about my world not being big enough to include you. I've known you close to ten years, and you've made your own place in my heart, whether it's the place you want to be or not."

"Then leave me alone, Damon."

"If that's what you really want, I'll have to respect that."

"It's what I want," she insisted. "I want to get on with my life."

"Then I wish you continued success in all your endeavors, DeAndra. Have a nice life."

Her voice had lost most of its edge. "You too, Damon. Bye."

When the phone clicked in his ear, Damon replaced the receiver, thinking about his options. He'd actually missed DeAndra and had no intention of giving up so easily. It wouldn't be smart to try to talk to DeAndra anymore, he decided, but for remainder of his trip to Washington, he would make sure he was visible and available. That meant adding the committee she was working with to his workload and making certain he took the same tours at the same time she did.

The plan wouldn't be difficult, he decided. His friend on the Congressional staff had really helped him by supplying him with the master list of committees, the rooms where they met, and the names of the participants.

When DeAndra replaced the receiver, Damon's words echoed in her thoughts. *"I've known you close to ten years, and you've made your own place in my heart, whether it's the place you want to be or not."*

Was it true? She didn't know what to believe because experience had taught her that love and desire could make a person believe anything. She'd been in Damon's life longer than any other woman had, but he hadn't really been seeing her as a woman until she forced the issue. Memories of the way she'd thrown herself at him still made her blush, but it had worked. They'd made love on several occasions. Surely he hadn't been fantasizing that she was really Imani the entire time, had he?

Shaking off that thought, she stretched out on the bed and closed her eyes. Damon was going to back off. This was a fact because he was a man of his word. What she couldn't figure was why she found no relief in the prospect.

Turning onto her side, she comforted herself with the conviction that things would be back to normal when she returned to Chicago and her position at the firm, her new condo, and her volunteer work at the legal aid center. Then she could put Damon Kessler at the very end of her "to do" list once more.

CHAPTER FOUR

Damon met Ben Walsh, a Congressional staffer and an old friend, for an early breakfast and to go over the schedule his staff had drawn up for Damon's Human Rights Summit meetings. Adjustments had been made to allow Damon to join more sessions with the up and coming lawyers.

"So which young lady are you interested in pursuing?" Ben asked, amusement sparkling in his eyes.

"It's not like that," Damon told him, his lips curving upward. "The young lady was one of my law clerks."

"Curiouser and curiouser." Ben lifted his fork and dug into his eggs scrambled with cheese. He was obviously waiting for Damon to explain.

"Not really," Damon said. "We weren't on good terms the last time I saw her and I've known her for years. We were good friends. I simply want the opportunity to set things straight."

"Uh huh." Ben shoveled more eggs into his mouth, chewed and swallowed. "You've still neglected to mention a name, but I scanned the list of promising young lawyers and one name stood out more than the others, DeAndra Blake. She's earning quite a reputation with her work at Hartfield, Merrien, and Sawyer. She's on the fast track to make partner. Damon, I used to think you might be hitting on her when we were in law school, but I couldn't believe you would be so reckless as to put your entire career in jeopardy. She was jailbait."

Damon shook his head. "No, I kept my head back then."

Though Ben's sharp brown eyes teemed with questions, Damon knew that he didn't want to explain what had happened. He was not an errant child, reporting to a parent. He was responsible for his own actions. "It's complicated," Damon said finally.

Ben swallowed. "Are you in love with her? After Imani…"

Damon cut in on him. "That was the problem. Look, Ben, I don't want to talk about it."

Ben nodded. "That's understandable. Damon, I'm going to say this, and then I'm going to mind my own business. Think twice before going after Ms. Blake. That girl loved you truly and deeply. That kind of love does not fade away. I often wondered if you felt something just as deep for her."

Yes, friendship, Damon answered in his thoughts. Something in Ben's comments bothered him. Reaching for the revised schedule that Ben's assistant had dropped off, he spoke in a confident tone. "I appreciate your concern and I'll think about what you said."

Ben inclined his head and leaned forward, changing the subject. "Hey, what do you think of those Pistons?"

Once the day officially started, Damon spent the first hour and a half scanning his committee's first draft of revised executive branch guidelines for human rights and United States assistance policies with international financial institutions. There were also accompanying suggested amendments to Title 22 of the United States Code.

Damon was fine-tuning the comments when a dark-haired young man in navy blue suit entered the room to stand beside his chair. When the young man cleared his throat, Damon gave him his attention.

"Excuse me Judge Kessler, sir. I'm Preston Williams, part of the group working on the rights of a child. According to the schedule, you will be joining us an hour from now. I'm here to inform you that we have reached a point where a senior review is required. Should you complete your current reviews earlier than expected, we would appreciate it if you'd join us immediately."

"Thank you." Damon put his pen down. "I'm almost done here." He checked his watch. "I should be there in about fifteen minutes."

The young man thanked him and left.

Damon opened the door to the conference room in time to hear a few lively remarks on children being forced into the military in several countries. DeAndra, who was speaking, looked up to see him in the doorway and stopped. Her large, golden brown eyes widened momentarily, and her ripe cherry-colored lips parted. Then the thick fringe of lashes dropped and she finished her statement.

The group facilitator stepped forward and initiated a round of introductions. When it was DeAndra's turn, she said, "We've already met. How are you, sir?"

In that moment, Damon was glad that he hadn't acknowledged her first and told everyone that she'd been his clerk. Ben's comments echoed in his head, making him question himself. What did he really want from DeAndra Blake? Only hours ago, the answered had seemed obvious. Now Damon wondered if he'd been fooling himself.

Following her lead, he answered, "I'm fine. It's good to see you again, DeAndra." He turned to the next person.

The group was made up of an equal number of legal professionals, Congressional staff members, and executive branch personnel from different federal agencies. They quickly provided Damon with a stack of papers that represented the group's output and decided that the most efficient way to proceed was for one of the group to brief him on the major points to facilitate his review. He agreed, and waited as they tried to decide who would brief him.

"DeAndra, I vote for you, since you're already acquainted with Judge Kessler," one of the other lawyers spoke up. Several other group members nodded in agreement.

The facilitator stood. "Is that all right with you, DeAndra?"

"Of course." Her face gave virtually nothing away. Only someone who knew her as well as he did would realize that the odd curve in her lush bottom lip meant she was biting it on the inside of her mouth.

"Judge Kessler?"

Damon smiled, deciding to give her an out. "I'm certain that any one of you could perform the task, so any selection made by the group is fine with me. I have no preferences."

The facilitator chose to ignore the gist of Damon's answer. He stood. "DeAndra is going to brief Judge Kessler on the group output and then he can perform his review. Everyone else in this group is free to take a time-out. We'll reconvene in a couple of hours." Tuning to Damon he asked, "Will two hours be enough?"

Damon scanned the stack. "It should be more than enough."

The room emptied rapidly as participants left for walks, office checks, phone calls, and the snack bar. Damon got up from his chair and went to the back of the room to fix himself a cup of coffee.

"Can I get you something?" he asked, looking at her as he stirred cream and sugar into his cup. He thought lavender designer suit was unusually beautiful on her. A floral print blouse with a ruffled collar that spilled out of the top of the zippered jacket softened the neckline, emphasizing her feminine features.

"No, I'm fine, thanks." Her voice was neutral. With her head tilted downward and her jaw set, she seemed determined to make the best of things.

Damon walked back to his chair and placed the coffee on the table. DeAndra was going through her copy of the various materials as he made himself comfortable in the chair. Positioning his stack of papers and appropriating one of the notepads scattered about the table, he glanced at her and said, "Anytime you're ready."

She began speaking in a clear, concise tone. Damon followed along, making notes on the pad. As she talked, she began to relax, the stiffness in her tone easing and emotion creeping in as she presented the group's views and suggestions for United States policy and enforcement relative to laws dealing with children's rights. It took a good forty minutes.

When she was done, Damon sat silent, considering her words. Then he inclined his head and drew his stack of papers closer. "Sounds like the group accomplished a lot."

"We did." DeAndra fiddled with her pencil. "A big goal with this group was to produce something that could inspire and initiate change in current U. S. policy and law."

"If this write-up is as good as your briefing, I'd say you have a good chance at succeeding," he said. "Thank you for briefing me."

"*Thank you*," she echoed. "Do you really think—"

Damon broke in quickly. "I really think there's a unique opportunity here and it seems that the group has done a fine job of capitalizing on it."

She nodded and took in a deep breath and let it out slowly. Then she pushed back her chair and stood. "I'll leave you to your review. I'll try to return at least twenty minutes early to answer any questions you might have."

"That would be fine. Until then…" Damon watched as she pushed her chair back into place. The short, pencil skirt fell an inch below the middle of her shapely thighs and hugged her rounded bottom as she headed for the door on two-inch heels. Damon forced himself to look away. He had no business ogling DeAndra's legs or her behind. It was not what he wanted from her.

In the empty room, Damon drank coffee and continued going over the group's output. It was as good as DeAndra's briefing had indicated. When DeAndra returned, he had his questions ready. She answered them clearly and concisely. Once or twice he caught himself staring at her, noticing her gorgeous skin, the darkness of her brows, the heavenly scent of her perfume. She stumbled over her words, knowledge of his scrutiny in her eyes. Then she moved on.

The rest of the group returned promptly to discuss changes. The session sailed along with the motivated group. It was almost one when they decided to break for a late lunch.

Damon sat silently, abruptly aware of what he had been doing with DeAndra. He'd been pursuing her, trying to be a part of her life as a man to a woman, despite the snow job he'd been giving himself. With Ben's words still echoing in the back of his thoughts, he chastised himself. Then he wondered if he could be around DeAndra without getting involved again.

Someone had made reservations for everyone at The Oceanaire. With some urging from the group, Damon tagged along, determined to keep his distance from the distracting DeAndra. Now that he'd finally gotten his life back in order, the last thing he needed was to get involved with DeAndra again.

Damon boarded the courtesy bus and took a seat right behind the driver. DeAndra found a seat in the middle where she sat and talked with two other women. At the seafood restaurant, they were given two leather booths with tables and chairs pushed together to make everyone fit.

Taking a seat at one end of the booth Damon watched the group jockey for positions next to friends, acquaintances, and people of influence. Two young lawyers took seats on his right. As Damon accepted a menu from the waiter, he saw DeAndra gracefully stepping towards the far end of the other side of the table.

In spite of himself, Damon breathed a low sigh of relief. Between Ben's comments and his own apparent inability to view DeAndra as simply another legal professional, he'd had enough. Yes, he wanted to patch things up with her and be friends again, but being around DeAndra was dangerous right now. He'd had only a casual fling in more than two years, and he was way too vulnerable. He couldn't keep his mind off her physical attributes. Getting the senior review position in her group had been a mistake.

"Judge Kessler," the heavyset young man in the herringbone suit began, "Alan Frye of Munson and Munson in Gary, Indiana. I've been following your cases closely. I was particularly interested in the case of Blaine Marshall and how he got to walk free after …"

A familiar wave of regret surged through Damon. That particular case had been haunting him for more years than he cared to count. The statement he always used when someone brought up the case came to his lips easily. "That was one of my least favorite cases," Damon said, opening his menu. "Unfortunately, the prosecution made several well documented errors that severely damaged their case. There was nothing I could do."

He scanned the menu, waiting for Frye to get the hint. On the other side of the table, they were shifting seats. Someone's fiancé had arrived and they were asking everyone to shift so that they could sit together. DeAndra somehow ended up right across from him.

Their gazes met and a sensual awareness sizzled between them. Pretending that it hadn't happened, Damon looked down to scan his menu. After a two-year hiatus, his hormones were leading him astray.

After a quick glance to confirm that no one else had noticed, DeAndra began to read her menu.

The waiter came around to take their orders. Several people ordered shrimp, shrimp scampi, halibut and stuffed gray sole with crabmeat, May shrimp and Brie cheese. Damon ordered jumbo lump crab cakes with mustard mayonnaise. When the food came, he virtually inhaled the crisp on the outside, moist and meaty on the inside, delicacies. Across from him, DeAndra struggled to eat the delicious but enormous fisherman's platter made up of fresh cod, shrimp, scallops and oysters with salt and vinegar fries. Several people in the group pitched in to help her.

After lunch, the group returned to their conference room to review the final drafts of their output. Then everyone left for the day.

DeAndra took the Metro back to the hotel stop and then walked back to her hotel. She'd been tired before, but now that Damon had joined the group, she was totally exhausted from trying to act as if he didn't affect her. It was a good thing that tomorrow was the final day. She'd felt hot and shaky the whole time she'd briefed him in the conference room and when she'd caught him staring, she'd stumbled with her words. No matter how much she hated to admit it, Damon Kessler still had a hold on her. She still loved him and it looked as though nothing was going to kill it. The thought was scary because she wasn't into wanting things that she couldn't have. She'd always been able to plot a path to the things she really wanted. Damon had been the exception.

She opened the door and the fragrance of exotic flowers filled her nostrils. The drapes were pulled back to fill the room with the setting sun. In her room, she kicked off her shoes and picked her way through the still beautiful flowers Damon had sent. Drawing back the covers, she sank down on the bed and stretched out on her back. *Get a grip girl. After tomorrow night, you can go back to your life in Chicago and never see him again.* That thought failed to comfort her. She wanted Damon, wished he were here right now to take her in his arms and make love to her. If only he could really love her. With a sigh, she turned over onto her side.

CHAPTER FIVE

Damon sat at the desk in his hotel room, reviewing some of the casework he'd brought along to insure that he didn't get too far behind in his work. The brief he'd just read had been horribly dry. He'd had to read it twice.

Taking off his glasses, he massaged the bridge of his nose and closed his eyes. He hadn't slept well last night so a full day in committees and groups had taken a toll. He'd done all that had been asked of him to the best of his ability, but he'd been distracted. DeAndra had been there, beautiful, smart, feminine, and sexy. Was it any wonder that he'd dreamed of her last night and the first time they'd made love?

Damon got up from the desk and pushed the chair back into place. His hands fisted. He was tired and definitely not himself. He reminded himself that he didn't want to remember being with DeAndra like that and he wanted her to forget too.

He glanced at his watch. In a couple of hours he would be attending the banquet and dinner dance signifying the end of the Human Rights Summit. He'd already given interviews discussing what he thought had been accomplished. Just talking about the issues and getting the right people to consider changes to current legislation and policies made everything worthwhile. He was proud to be a part of the summit and everything they'd tried to accomplish.

In the small but luxurious bedroom, he removed the black tux he would wear tonight from his closet. He'd purchased a fancy white dress shirt to go with it and his black dress shoes had been shined to perfection. Placing his gold and black cuff links on the nightstand, he drew back the covers on the bed and stretched out on the starched sheets.

Gradually, he sank into the depths of sleep.

Hours later, he stood in the open doorway of his friend and date for the evening, the pretty and vivacious Judge Nelda Hawker's room, offering her a white box tied with a satin ribbon. He'd just complimented her on her floor length watered silk gown with the antique roses bordering the bottom and the side slits that emphasized her shapely legs.

She thanked him for the compliment, her obvious pleasure in opening the box and drawing out the white orchid corsage made him smile. "Thank you, Damon. It's gorgeous!" She flashed white, even teeth, and dimples.

"Help me put it on," she directed, her big brown eyes sparkling. "I feel like I'm going to the prom all over again."

"Me too," Damon said, "but every time I get a glimpse of this stuff in the mirror, reality sets in." He fingered the white hair that touched his temples.

"It's just a little bit, Damon, and it makes you look so distinguished. You're already a handsome devil!" Nelda laughed and gathered him into her arms. "Thanks for the corsage. I'm going to treasure it and this moment."

Her arms tightened around him and her soft lips brushed his cheek. When she glanced back at him, wiping her lipstick off his cheek with a fingertip, there was an invitation in those eyes.

"Nelda, you're very welcome," he answered, carefully ignoring the invitation in her eyes. "I'm looking forward to enjoying the banquet with you."

"Good. Let's get this pinned on my dress." She lifted one of the white watered silk straps criss-crossing her full breasts and waited expectantly.

With an expertise gained from pinning corsages on Imani and DeAndra numerous times, he bent to the task, his fingers carefully avoiding the curvaceous expanse of rich, chocolate colored skin. Nelda was very attractive, but his hormones were not leaping at the prospect. Sliding the pin in and out of the fabric, he finished quickly.

"Thank you." Nelda retrieved a beaded silk purse and wrap from the coffee table. "Shall we go?"

Together they left the room and took the elevator to the lobby level. Then they followed the crowd of attendees in formal attire down a long hallway to the Presidential Ballroom.

Inside the blue-walled room, decorated with antebellum style cornices, drapery, and woodwork reminiscent of The White House, they greeted several friends and acquaintances. Damon introduced Nelda to his old college roommate, Colton Roberts and his wife, Tiffany, and to Ben. Then they worked the crowd and drank cocktails. Damon made it a point to stop and chat with some of the people who had been instrumental in him getting his position in the court.

Peering through the crowd, he was surprised that he didn't even catch a glimpse of DeAndra. He decided that it was probably for the best, but continued to look for her anyway.

"Who are you looking for?" Nelda asked, glancing in the direction he'd been looking in.

"No one in particular, just some of the young lawyers who were part of my sessions." Damon took her hand and led her toward their assigned table. He could see that Ben was already seated there.

"You'll probably see a lot of them after dinner," Nelda said, leaning closer. "They've arranged for three different bands and one was picked just for the younger set."

"And what do they have for the older set, Lawrence Welk's Champagne Bubble Music?" Damon quipped.

Nelda laughed. "No silly, we're not *that* old. They have a top forties band and a rhythm and blues band."

Dinner was a grand and delicious affair with prime rib, tropical garden salad, green beans with almonds, and garlic roasted potatoes. The lights were turned off when it was time for dessert and an audible sigh filled the air when the wait staff entered the ballroom with flaming Cherries Jubilee. Nelda and Damon savored their food and enjoyed themselves.

Once the tables were cleared, there was a short ceremony where all the attendees were thanked for donating their time and efforts. At the end of the program, the first band, the Monarchs, was introduced. Their first song was a rousing rendition of *Shake Your Booty*. After that, Nelda insisted that Damon dance the next dance with her. It was a lively version of *Celebration Time*.

Damon got on the dance floor with Nelda and moved, stepped, and spun through several songs. Chugging and swinging her arms, Nelda swiveled her hips and executed some fancy footwork.

Damon and Nelda were in the middle of a slow dance when he spotted DeAndra near the edge of the dance floor in the arms of a young lawyer he recognized as the prosecuting attorney for a case where a famous baseball player had been accused of killing his wife. The two of them laughed and talked as they danced.

The sight of DeAndra in the other man's arms disturbed Damon, but he couldn't look away. He had no right to feel this way. His need to see DeAndra to resolve the issues between them, and his inability to keep his thoughts on an appropriate level in her presence, were all proof that things were a lot more complicated than he had ever imagined.

Nelda turned her head and followed the direction of his gaze. "Who's that?"

Damon replied in an even tone, "One of the lawyers from my sessions and that young prosecuting attorney who headed the Smithfield case."

"I remember. He did an excellent job." Nelda watched them for a moment and then turned back to smile at him. "See? Didn't I say that you'd probably see the younger people once the music started?"

Feeling as if he'd just been reminded of his age, Damon inclined his head. "Yes, you did."

She tightened her fingers on his. "That's a cute couple!"

Damon said nothing as he turned them on a circle so that DeAndra and her friend were no longer in view. After that, he made a determined effort to focus on Nelda.

By the time the band was two-thirds through their performance, Nelda was dragging. "I had a long day," she explained with an apologetic smile. "I'm going to call it a night. Walk me back to the room, Damon."

"Of course." He drew her silk wrap from the back of the chair and placed it on her shoulders. Then taking her arm, he led the way out of the ballroom.

As they stood outside Nelda's room, she fished in her bag for the key. Fitting the card into the slot, she watched the indicator turn green as the lock clicked. Turning the knob, she opened the door. "Come in for a minute."

Damon hesitated for a moment. He knew what was coming and he wasn't going into that minefield. When Nelda lifted a brow, he stepped into the room without a word.

When the door closed behind him, Nelda put her arms around him and leaned close to kiss his cheek. "I really enjoyed myself these evening, Damon, thank you."

He met her gaze, his arms tightening and then releasing her in a hug. "I had a blast too. We've got to do it again sometime."

She leaned close again, this time her soft lips brushed his, once, twice. "Stay with me, Damon, I'll make it real good for you," she said in a soft, husky voice.

"I'm sure you would," he answered, his tone gentle. "But I can't."

Nelda leaned into him so that her lush breasts touched his chest. Her eyes searched his face, her gaze provocative. "It's been a long time Damon, for both of us. There'd be no strings attached."

"Yes, there would." Damon stepped back, putting more distance between them. He'd experienced an instinctive response, but it paled in comparison to the way he'd been feeling with DeAndra in the same room all day. "Nelda, we're friends, so whatever we'd do would involve more than giving each other a little comfort. I value our friendship. I'm not going there, so give up gracefully."

"All right, Damon." She smoothed the pout of her lips into a semblance of a smile, but her eyes were shiny with moisture. "I guess I'll have to accept that."

Damon kissed her cheek once more. "Thanks again, Nelda. Check me out the next time you're in the Detroit area."

"I will." Nelda gripped his hand. "Take care, Damon."

Acknowledging her comment with a squeeze of her hand, he exited the room. He was in the elevator, on the way to his room when he realized that he did not want to be alone. He realized that in his current state, it would be better to sit in the ballroom, chat with old friends and new acquaintances, and enjoy the music than to sit in the room and stew over Nelda's offer. Damon hit the button for the lobby level.

When he arrived back at the ballroom, he saw that a number of people had left, but a sizeable crowd remained. Not seeing any of his friends among the people sitting at the tables or along the sides of the dance floor, he scanned the dancers. He recognized no one.

Damon went back to the empty table and ordered a shot of cognac. The second band, The Kaylets, was in the middle of their performance. Relaxing in his chair, he drank his cognac and listened to the music.

"Did your date retire for the night?"

Turning at the sound of the voice, he looked up to see DeAndra standing at his table in a glittery black evening gown reminiscent of the flapper style. The front was a short, flirty length that tastefully displayed her beautiful legs, but the back was a strappy affair on top, with a skirt that hugged her hips and ended at the tops of her shimmering heels. Recovering from his shock, he answered, "Yes, Nelda was tired.

What about your date?"

"Aubrey has to catch an early flight home," she explained.

Damon pushed one of the chairs away from the table. "Won't you join me?"

Their gazes locked and then she answered, "Yes." DeAndra put her glass of wine on the table and sat down next to him.

"I'm glad to have this chance to talk before we get on a plane and go our separate ways," he said.

"Me too." DeAndra swallowed. "I know I haven't made it easy. What did you want to say?"

Damon stared into her beautiful brown eyes. "First, my conscience compels me to apologize for pushing so hard to get back into your life. You did a masterful job of keeping me at bay."

"Really?" She played with the stem of her glass, uncertainty and longing in her eyes. "Then why have I been such a basket case this week? Maybe I should have just gone with the flow."

Damon leaned closer. "There's nothing wrong with trying to keep yourself from getting hurt."

"Maybe not, Damon, but I spent a lot of time pushing you away and saying no, when I really wanted to say yes."

"Are you saying yes, now?"

Her eyes widened. "I don't know."

"And that's okay." He took her soft hand and squeezed it. "I really thought what I was doing was all about an apology and being friends again. Yesterday I realized that it's a lot more complicated."

"How complicated?" she asked softly, her gaze for him alone.

"I've missed you and I want to be friends again, but…"

"But?" she mocked him gently.

Setting his jaw, he let the words tumble out. "I'm much too attracted to you and I don't even want to think about getting involved with anyone right now, not when I'm enjoying my life again."

Bottomless brown eyes regarded him silently. Then her lips spread into a tremulous smile. "Thank you for sharing."

She raised the glass of wine to her lips to sip. Damon eyed the luscious curve of her lips as she swallowed, wondering what it would be like to kiss them, now that his heart and mind were free of Imani.

When she'd set the glass back onto the table, she extended a hand. "Let's dance, Damon. Who knows when we'll see each other again? Tomorrow we'll go back to our separate lives."

The band began to play their version of Lionel Ritchie's "Three Times a Lady." Taking her hand, he led her to the floor and pulled her into his arms. She laid her head on his chest and her scent tantalized him. The warmth of her body seemed to penetrate his suit. With every step, his legs brushed hers. His hand, at her waist touched the silky skin of her back through the decorative straps.

Sensual currents of emotion and desire rushed through him, heating his body, and making him feel more vulnerable and alive then he'd felt in years. He held on, moving around the dance floor as though nothing had happened.

With the large number of people slow dancing and remaining on the floor, the band played two additional slow dances. Damon and DeAndra danced them all. By the third dance, they were both shaking.

DeAndra slowly pulled away, her provocative scent still filling his nostrils. "I think I'll call it a night," she said as they walked away from the other couples.

Damon found himself reluctant to end their time together. He'd been enjoying himself. When the band began a rendition of a Kool and the Gang party song, he turned back for the dance floor. "One last dance," he urged.

"All right, Damon." She followed him back, already starting her dance.

The music changed their mood and switched their focus to performing all the old dances that people used to do. When it was over, they left the left the floor together to exit the ballroom.

"I really am calling it a night this time," she said a little breathlessly.

Damon chuckled. "I won't argue with you. Just let me escort you back to your room."

At her nod, they took the hallway and climbed onto the elevator. Upstairs, outside her door, Damon waited while she fitted her card into the lock and opened the door. Turning to face him in the opening, she waited, her brown eyes luminous.

In a heartbeat he had her in his arms, her lush curves burning holes in his tux. When his mouth came down on those soft, sweet lips, she opened for him with a little gasp. Damon drank from her mouth, sliding his tongue against hers, and savoring her sweetness.

She kissed him back, her tongue thrusting and playing with his as one soft hand slid up his neck to massage his nape and the other cupped the side of his face.

Sliding his hands down to her waist, he stopped short of her hips. He could feel her body trembling against him. Fire and desire ripped through his body, threatening to overwhelm and leaving a deep ache. He released her abruptly.

Both struggled to catch their breath. Proof of his vulnerability, the kiss disturbed him. It was a good thing they were going back to different cities. Noting the shiny glint in DeAndra's eyes, Damon searched for the right words to say.

"Good night," she said, her voice just above a whisper. "Have a safe trip home."

"You too. Good night," he echoed as she nodded, then closed and locked the door.

In a daze, Damon stood in the hall for several moments. Deep inside he wanted to knock on the door and join DeAndra inside, but common sense prevailed. Sleeping with DeAndra would pull him deep into the fire. He was still smarting from the last time he'd gotten burned.

CHAPTER SIX

DeAndra was glad to board the plane for Chicago the next morning. She hadn't slept much. She spent most of the night rerunning the time spent with Damon and wondering if she should have handled him differently. When she'd left two years ago, she given up all hope of being with him, but despite her best efforts, she still loved Damon.

On the crowded plane, she stared out the window at the blue sky filled with fluffy white clouds and her heart filled with hope and determination. She would get through this.

Back in Chicago, she retrieved her luggage, then her car. On her way home, she stopped at the office in a move born out of sheer self-preservation. The firm had gotten one of the other associates to handle DeAndra's most important cases while she was gone, but there was still a lot of work to do.

As she was going through her stack of files in her little cubbyhole of an office, Len Sawyer, one of the partners in Hartfield, Merrien, and Sawyer stopped in to welcome her back. He was in his forties and immaculately groomed. His brown hair was expensively cut and the custom-made herringbone suit he wore covered any imperfections in his six-foot frame.

"DeAndra, you did an excellent job of representing the firm," he said after dispensing with the pleasantries. "Your testimony before Congress was moving and skillfully researched and delivered. The qualities you displayed are some of the most important in what we look for in junior partners."

DeAndra worked hard to maintain her cool. She'd promised herself that she wouldn't get too excited if the partners got complimentary on her work in Washington but now her pulse was already speeding up, hope filling her chest. "Will what I did at the summit have any impact on the upcoming selections for junior partners?"

Brown eyes practically melting, Sawyer flashed her a patronizing smile that DeAndra equated to a pat on the head. It was a look male associates would never see. Her smile faded as she concentrated on what he was saying.

"No, DeAndra. I'm sorry, but the selections for junior partner have already been made. As you know, we look at our tenured associates every five years. You haven't been with us long enough to qualify."

"I see." DeAndra struggled to hide the sinking feeling inside her. She'd done a lot work for the firm, including some of the most challenging cases. The work had brought her into contact with all of the partners.

Sawyer extended his smooth, soft hand to give hers a limp shake. "I just wanted to say we're proud of you. Keep up the good work."

Thanking him, DeAndra was glad when he finally left. She'd known in her heart that it was too soon for her to make partner, but she'd hoped just the same.

Shaking off her disappointment, she drank a Pepsi and went back to work. Reviewing the casework that had been done, she made a schedule of depositions to be taken and motions to be filed. It was eight in the evening when she left the office.

Because he'd stayed in Washington longer than he'd originally planned, Damon had to fly standby, but nevertheless managed to get a seat in first class. He used the flight to mentally tick off the successes of his trip. He'd had a chance to hobnob with the president and some of his advisors, and he'd also made the most of an opportunity to address Congress and work with its staff. Hopefully that experience plus his influential friends and his record would get him on the list of possible presidential appointees to the circuit court. He didn't allow himself to think about DeAndra and what had happened and hadn't happened between them because his feelings for her obviously involved more than he was prepared to deal with.

The flight arrived in Detroit at one-thirty in the afternoon and as he waited for his luggage to roll by on the carousel in baggage claim, he saw that it was a bright and sunny day. The urge to take advantage of it by accepting a friend's invitation to go out on his boat pulled at Damon, but the sense of duty associated with the pile of work he knew waited for him at the office was too strong. Instead of calling his secretary to get a status on his calls and correspondence, he decided to drop by the office.

When he stepped into the cool blue interior of his outer office, he found Tori busy filing.

"Hey, welcome back, Judge Kessler!" she beamed, looking up from an open drawer in the filing cabinet. "The package you left went to Chief Clay's office by courier the day you left for Washington. I took vacation time for most of the time you were gone, but when you said you were coming back to Detroit today or tomorrow, and Caline called to tell me that we had a bunch of mail, I decided to come in and get things ready. Good thing I did, because the pile of mail was pretty high."

Returning her smile, Damon let the heavy wooden door close behind him. "Thanks for the welcome. It's always good to come home. Anything pressing right now?"

Tori shrugged, her ponytail swinging. "Just the usual, but you did get some personal mail."

Personal mail? He didn't like the sound of that. Damon strode to the door of his private office and opened it.

Tori followed him inside. There were three piles in the middle of his desk. "Case info, solicitations, and personal," she said, pointing each out. There was only one letter in the personal pile.

Shrugging out of his gray suit jacket, he flipped a switch and hung it in the closet hidden in the oak paneling. Then he settled into his cushioned leather chair, contemplating the letter in front of him. As before, it was unstamped and the words *Private* were scrolled across the front of a personal-sized envelope in black ink letters.

"Another letter from your secret admirer?" Tori asked, still hovering in his office.

The last thing he wanted was to drag Tori into the mess. The less she knew, the better. "That'll be all, Tori." Raising his brows, Damon gave her the no nonsense facial expression.

"Yes, sir." She looked disappointed as she turned to walk out, closing the door behind her.

Damon opened a drawer in his desk, pulled out a pair of vinyl gloves, and slipped them on. Fleetingly, he considered adding a mask for his nose and then laughed at himself. Things had not progressed that far and probably never would. He used the letter opener to carefully slit open the envelope. Retrieving the folded paper inside, he read the message:

Darling,

Don't say I didn't warn you. By running off without even so much as a goodbye-bye you've made me very angry. You bad boy! I couldn't believe you would treat me this way. Now you've got to take the bad with the good. I was FURIOUS. I guess you can tell. (smile) It's all your fault for not considering my feelings. The things you do for love! If you're not back soon, I'm not responsible for my actions. See ya, lover, hopefully tomorrow morning, same place, same time.

Jalanna

Damon stared at the letter. There was an implied threat. No, the letter implied that something had been done, he decided. What did this Jalanna mean when she said she guessed he could tell? There'd been nothing harmful in the envelope and his office was immaculate. He stood a moment to check the side window for a glimpse of his Benz. It was just the way he'd left it.

Still puzzling over the letter and trying to ignore the cold, creepy feeling inching up the back of his neck, Damon dialed Warfield Clay's private line and got the answering machine. Leaving a short message in which he promised to send the latest letter over by courier, Damon settled down to work.

Fifteen minutes later, he realized that he was still on the same page. The letter had him too wound up. He culled the most important files into a stack and stuffed them into his briefcase. Then he gave Tori the sealed package for the courier and told her that he'd decided to work from home.

Tori studied the sealed package and then glanced back at Damon. "Could you let me in on what's going on? You seem a little upset and I'm thinking it has something to do with the personal mail you received."

Damon scanned her face, trying to decide if he should bring her into his confidence. Reasoning that she had to handle his mail and his calls and was therefore in a certain amount of danger too, he made a decision. He set his briefcase on the floor. "Tori, I've been getting mail that has threatening overtones. The letters started out pleasantly enough, but now they're somewhat ominous. I don't now who's writing them and I don't think it's anyone I've met. The letters imply that the writer is someone who observes me on my daily morning run."

"Wow!" Tori's eyes went wide. "Do you ever look at the people on your daily run?"

Damon gave her a patient smile. "No. At least I didn't until the letters started to sound more like threats. Since then, I've never seen the same person twice. But think about it. If you were going to threaten someone and reveal that you watched at a certain time or place daily, wouldn't you take steps to conceal your identity?"

"I guess so." Tori's eyes were full of sympathy. "What do you want me to do?"

Damon sighed. "Just be extra careful when you handle the mail. Don't tell *anyone* about my plans and whereabouts without my specific okay, and notify me immediately when unstamped personal mail arrives."

"I'll do that Judge Kessler. You can count on me, sir."

"Thank you, Tori." As Damon lifted his briefcase, the phone rang. He waited as Tori answered and asked the caller to hold on for a moment.

"It's Chief Clay," she said. "Do you want to take it in your office?"

"No, this is fine." He took the receiver. "Clay? So you got my message? No, the letter hasn't gone out yet. Yes, I'll bring it over. I was just leaving anyway. Yes, see you then, bye." Replacing the receiver, he gave Tori his attention once more. "Tori…"

"Sir, you don't have to worry about me. All your information is now top secret."

Suppressing a smile, Damon said, "Tori, let's back that down to classified, meaning information will be disseminated on a need-to-know basis only, okay?"

"Yes sir!" The ponytail swung from side to side.

Lifting the briefcase once more, Damon left the office. He scanned the immediate area as he walked to his car, a nervous energy driving him. He unlocked the door and opened it carefully, the entire time wondering if the car would explode, blowing him to bits. The hardest thing he had to do was to shut the door, fit his key into the lock, and start the car. He was actually sweating by the time he'd started the engine and put the car into gear. Switching on the air full blast, he realized that he could not go on like this. If Clay didn't do something soon, he was going to hire a bodyguard.

At the police station downtown, he parked his car in the visitors lot and made his way back to Clay's office. His friend was at his desk, going through a stack of crime scene photos while he chomped steadily on an unlit cigar. He apparently hadn't kicked the cigar habit yet.

"Hello, Clay, good to see you, buddy."

"Good to see you're still kickin'." Clay stood up to take his hand and shake it while they patted each other on the back in a brotherly hug. "Man, it sounds like your stalker's getting serious. Have a seat."

Damon gave him the package. "This is the letter. Clay, you've got to do something. I had a hard time just opening the door to my car and starting it up for the drive over here. I guess I've seen too many action flicks with exploding cars."

"Never underestimate the power of being paranoid," Clay said, placing the cigar in a crystal ashtray. "It could save your life." He drew a file from his *In* box. "Let me fill you in on what we've done so far. Each letter was checked for fingerprints, but we found none. Your stalker obviously wears gloves when she prepares each letter. We've determined that the person who wrote the letters is right-handed." Clay drummed his fingers on his desk. "As far as you're concerned, you've never seen this person face-to-face. I've already assigned an undercover officer to follow you on your morning run and note anything suspicious. To help the investigation along, we can install a hidden camera near the place where your mail arrives so we can get a picture of your stalker making the delivery. Do you know what time mail is delivered to your office?"

Damon shrugged. "Sometime before ten-thirty."

"We'll find out for sure." Clay reclined back in his chair, rubbing his top lip with a forefinger. "By the way, I've got something you can use. We'll set up one of those little spy cameras tonight. Feel better?"

"A little, but I'm seriously thinking of getting a bodyguard," Damon admitted. "I don't like looking over my shoulder all the time."

"Dennis will be guarding you on the morning run." Clay drew out a pair of gloves and slipped them on. "Let me review the latest letter."

Drawing the white, folded sheet of paper from the envelope, he smoothed it out and scanned it for several moments. His jaw tightened as he refolded the sheet and placed it back inside the envelope. "This thing is escalating."

"Yeah." Damon ran a hand over his eyes. He'd seen the deep concern in his friend's eyes and it was making him nervous.

Clay's voice held an edge of warning. "This letter indicates that *something* was done. You checked your car and the office and everything is okay?"

"Yeah, everything was fine," Damon confirmed.

"Have you been home yet?"

"No, I went from the airport to the office." Standing, Damon felt a swirling in the pit of his stomach. "I think I should go home now."

Clay retrieved the cigar and stuffed it in his mouth. "Damn straight. Hold up for a moment and I'll introduce you to Dennis. Then we can all go check out your place."

Ten minutes later, Damon was in his car and on his way home. Behind him, in an unmarked patrol car, Clay and undercover officer Errol Davis followed.

When he finally pulled into his garage, he actually had to force himself to behave normally. By the time he got of the car and retrieved his briefcase, Clay and Davis had parked in front of the house and were walking towards him.

For Damon, the bright sunny day had taken on an ominous feel. He found that he couldn't enjoy the fact that he'd finally made it home after being gone for days. Leading them up the steps, he stopped at the door to remove his keys from a pants pocket.

"You won't be needing your key," Clay said.

At his words, Damon's head whipped up. He saw that his front door was ajar.

"Let us go first," Clay said, moving forward with Davis. "Someone might still be in there."

In mute agreement, Damon stepped aside. He saw both men draw their guns.

"We'll tell you when it's safe to come in," Davis whispered as he went past and entered.

The back of Damon's neck prickled as he stood on the porch listening hard. He didn't feel safe. Any minute, his crazed intruder could come running out to attack him. Maybe his stalker was hiding nearby and watching everything.

He strained his ears. No sound reached him except for the occasional crunch of glass underfoot. He imagined that all his crystal collection had been smashed.

Damon felt as if he'd been standing on the porch an hour before Clay called that it was safe for him to come in. He went in cautiously, not taking many steps before he was stepping on broken glass. He'd been right about the crystal.

"Don't touch anything," Clay said, coming from the kitchen, "and brace yourself. Whoever did this is sick."

Damon's jaw tightened as he went into the great room. What he saw filled him with an impotent mix of anger and awe. His beautiful, imported cream couch had been ripped and shredded with a knife and someone had splattered blood all over it. Tables were overturned, some broken. Obscenities written with black and red markers covered his walls.

"Take a look at the bedroom," Davis said, coming up from the basement.

Wondering how his bedroom could look any worse than what he'd seen in the great room, Damon went to take a look. What he saw stopped him at the door.

Torn rags and strips of material littered the floor, the remains of his clothes. At a loss for words, he stared, wondering what drove a twisted mind to do something like this. They'd taken his home and made it something ugly and perverse. They'd taken it from him. Looking around, Damon knew he would never feel the same about this place.

A small puddle of what appeared to be dried blood crowned the center of his white Egyptian cotton sheets and the yellow stain of urine colored the pillows. All of his picture frames were bent and broken, the pictures ripped, twisted, and trampled on.

Damon rescued the picture of his father from the mess on the floor and sadly smoothed it out. It was his favorite picture of his Dad and had been taken shortly before he'd died.

The writing in red lipstick on the full-length mirror near the bed drew his attention:

I bleed; my heart bleeds because of what you've done to me. You don't deserve me, but I still love you anyway. Take this for what it is, my way of showing you that I am **serious** *about you.* **Don't play with my heart!**

Jalanna

Damon heard approaching footsteps and the crunching sound of glass underfoot. It was Clay. "You're in serious danger here. I think you should take those bags you've got in the car and head back to the airport. This chick is wacko, if she really is a chick. These days you never know who or what you're dealing with! I'll get a team in here and we'll analyze everything, look for prints, check out that stuff that looks like dried blood. We'll also interview the neighbors and see if anyone heard anything."

Damon was silent as he glanced around the room one last time.

Clay put a heavy hand on Damon's shoulder and squeezed. "I'm sorry, but you can't stay here, man," Clay said, emphasizing his point.

"That wasn't in my plan," Damon said, turning away from the ruins of his bedroom. "I don't think I belong here anymore. How long should I stay away from Detroit?"

Clay shrugged, his eyes troubled. "Give me two months. We'll keep in touch. Do you know where you're going?"

Damon racked his brain and came up short. "No, but a few of my friends should be able to help me out. If not, I should be able to take an extended vacation somewhere pleasant."

The men walked to the front door. Davis was already there, waiting. "Give me a note for your secretary," Clay ordered, pulling the door open. "I don't want you to have contact with her or anyone else around here. I'll talk to her. Transfer or put your legal cases on hold for now. None of that stuff is worth your life."

In mute acknowledgement, Damon fished for his key. "How are you going to catch this Jalanna?"

"Good police work," Davis put in.

"We also have someone in the department who looks enough like you to be your brother. We might be able to use him to catch your stalker," Clay added.

"I hope it doesn't come to that," Damon said, stepping out from behind Clay and Davis. "I wouldn't want anyone to get hurt or killed because of me."

"Hey, cut out the negative thinking," Clay cautioned. "I'm worried about you, man. You do what you have to do and don't come back here until we give the okay."

Damon nodded as he closed the door and locked it with his key. "I think you'll need this," he said, placing his key in Clay's palm.

"Thanks." Clay shook his hand and patted his shoulder. "Take care of yourself, buddy."

Clay and Davis retrieved crime scene tape from the trunk of their car and taped off the house. Then they called for an investigative team.

Damon made a point of driving off when Clay and Davis did, but he didn't know where he was going. A numbness had his thoughts cycling endlessly and kept him from making a plan. Finally he ended up at the house of his surgeon friend, Cotter Eastwood, in Grosse Point Shores. This time the gorgeous view of the shore of Lake St. Clair failed to move him.

He found Cotter in the spacious backyard in his chef hat by the grill, putting the finishing touches on some ribs before he took off for the marina. "Hey Damon, glad to see you're back from D.C.," Cotter said, looking up from the grill. "Have a seat. I'll be ready to leave in a minute."

"I won't be able to go out on the boat today." Damon dropped down into one of the fancy chairs. "In fact, I should be leaving in the next couple of hours."

Cotter put down the tongs and faced him. "Damon, you look like a man who could use a drink."

"You got that right."

"What'll you have? Want a black Russian?"

"Yes, you know how I like it. I'll keep an eye on your grill."

While his friend fixed his drink, Damon listened to the quiet sizzle of the meat on the grill and the normal sounds of the neighborhood, but none of it seemed real. His day was no longer normal.

Cotter was quick with the drink. "What's up, buddy?" he asked, taking the seat next to Damon. "You look whipped."

"Man, I feel whipped. I just came from my house and it's been trashed. I've got a stalker and the threats are escalating. Clay wants me to get out of town now and I think he's right."

"Man!" The little shake of Cotter's head and his widened eyes underscored his amazement. "Where are you gonna go?"

"I don't know. My mind's drawing a blank right now. I was hoping you could help me." Damon gulped the drink. He knew that alcohol wasn't the answer to anything, but dammit, he needed this one.

"If I were you, I'd go someplace like the Virgin Islands or Hawaii, but if you want someplace quieter and not so far away while you're laying low, I have a house in Chicago that you could use. I turned it into condos and kept one for my personal use. I used to go there all the time to get away from my family. For a while, I thought I was actually going to move there."

Damon made a point of ignoring his friend's remark about his family. Cotter came from a family with old money and they were as snobby as could be. They'd cost him numerous relationships and were always trying to run his life. Before Cotter had wised up and learned to keep them out of his personal business, he'd lost his fiancée, Mariah McCleary.

"So, think you might like to lay low in Chicago?"

Damon liked Chicago. When he'd had more of a social life, he'd spent many weekends there. "Sounds like a good idea. Is your condo empty?"

"Yes, you lucky dog. I just had it redecorated because I've been thinking of selling it. Let me get the key."

"Just like that?" Damon asked.

"Yes, just like that. What are friends for?" Cotter was up and back in the house before Damon could think of a reply.

When Cotter reappeared, he had the keys, a map, and some Yahoo directions. Damon thanked him profusely and then at Cotter's urging, left for Chicago.

CHAPTER SEVEN

Finishing some paperwork at the neighborhood legal clinic, DeAndra put her pencil down for the tenth time and glanced toward the hall. Where was Mouse? She missed her little buddy. Mouse loved helping out at the legal center and generally hanging around. It wasn't like her to stay away without a very good reason. DeAndra missed the child's chatter, her sassy personality, her interest in everything, and her warm heart. DeAndra had a little present in her bag, just waiting for Mouse.

Standing up to stretch, she walked out to the hall. Four people were waiting patiently, but there were no volunteers at the clinic to get them started. DeAndra ducked back into the office, grabbed the intake forms the office used and a handful of pens. Back in the hall, she gave each prospective client a pen and a form attached to a clipboard. This was the sort of thing at which Mouse excelled. Sighing, and deciding that this was as good a time as any to take a break, DeAndra closed the door to the office, told everyone she was taking a little break, and took off.

Outside the old brick building, she sat in a lawn chair under the old maple tree and people-watched under the beady eye of the security guard. She hadn't been sitting there more than five minutes when she saw Mouse's friend Rico coming up the street on his bike with his natural hair standing out like he was one of the Jackson Five. He usually stopped to talk with DeAndra and Mouse, but today he seemed to be concentrating on riding his bicycle.

"Hey Rico, what's up?" she called with a smile.

Rico skidded to a stop and climbed down off the seat. "Hi, Ms. Blake. 'Chelle said you were in Washington, D.C. Did you get to meet the president? How was it?"

"I didn't meet the president, but it was great. I even got to be on television for a little while."

Rico used his handlebars to turn his front wheel from side to side. "I heard about that. Chelle said her momma taped it."

"Speaking of Mouse," DeAndra said using her nickname for Michelle and making a show of looking up and down the block, "have you seen her?"

Rico's entire demeanor changed. His forehead wrinkled and he suddenly found the ground very interesting.

DeAndra decided to wait him out. He was not going to take off on that bike without telling her something. "Rico?"

His face came up, various expressions warring with each other. DeAndra read fear, confusion, and a need to confide in someone. An icy finger of foreboding touched her and she pushed it away in the warm sunshine. "You can tell me," she added softly.

"Something bad happened and she runned away," Rico declared.

"Something bad?" The icy finger came back to settle on the back of her neck. DeAndra examined the words in her mind, trying to squeeze more information out of them. "*What* happened?"

Rico's shoulders went up and down and his head swiveled from one side to the other. "I don't know."

Something in his dark eyes made DeAndra suspect that he did. After all, Rico and Mouse were good friends. Her eyes narrowed. "Rico…"

"I don't know!" he insisted.

"Then where is she now?"

"I don't know!" Rico's shrill voice pierced the air. "And that's what I told her mom and her uncle. Dang! It ain't fair. She runs away and everybody thinks I know something about it!"

Rico jumped back on the bike and pedaled away fast.

Something had put the fear of God in that child. Watching him,

DeAndra prayed. *Dear lord, please don't let anything have happened to Mouse.* She shivered, certain there was a cloud in front of the bright afternoon sun.

She fought a powerful urge to go to Mouse's house right now and get to the truth behind the things Rico had said, but caution and her responsibility to help the clients waiting inside the center held her in place. All she had was some wild statements from a child. Neither the newspapers she'd read nor the newscasts she'd watched had mentioned a newly missing child.

Back inside, DeAndra checked the sign up list and called the next client, an elderly man who was having problems with his landlord. Before long, she was delving deep into his problems.

By the time she finished doing intake and whatever she could for the day for each client, it was nearly seven. As she gathered her briefcase and purse, DeAndra dropped back into her chair and picked up the phone. Before she knew what she was doing, she'd dialed Mouse's house. Sonia answered in a strained voice.

DeAndra spoke into the receiver, trying to make her voice sound as normal as possible. "Sonia, this is DeAndra. Is Mouse at home? I didn't see her at the center today."

Sonia hesitated for a long moment, causing DeAndra's fears to escalate. When Sonia spoke, her voice seemed unnaturally low. "She…she somewhere in the neighborhood. I don't think she knows you're back."

The silence stretched on forever. "Will you let her call me when she gets in?" DeAndra asked, aiming for peace of mind.

"Sure," Sonia's voice was almost normal now. "It should be in about an hour."

So, according to Sonia, Mouse was home and hanging in the neighborhood. DeAndra hung up the phone, grabbed her things, and headed for her car, all the while cursing her suspicious nature. She wanted to believe Sonia, but something deep inside her suspected that the woman had lied.

Tired and hungry, DeAndra picked up a salad and headed home. To silence the inner voice, she even drove through Mouse's neighborhood and past her house. A few neighborhood children were out playing, but there was no sign of her little friend. With a prayer on her lips, DeAndra went home, feeling helpless.

DeAndra got up early on Sunday, dressed, and went to the early church service. Her minister, Pastor Avers, was so proud of her and the work she'd done in Washington that he recognized her in front of the congregation. They gave her a standing ovation. The sermon centered on treating everyone as equals, a theme that encompassed human rights.

After church, she went to breakfast at her favorite little Coney Island. It was basically a hole in the wall, but it was a warm and friendly place where everyone became part of an extended family and the food was wonderful. Over a ham and cheese omelet and coffee, she caught up on gossip and listened to the old timers argue about the previous night's fight.

As DeAndra headed home, the older, stately homes with the landscaped yards gave way to smaller, aluminum and wood framed structures. Several were quite run down. Some cried out for a fresh coat of paint. It seemed natural that she should again end up in Mouse's neighborhood. Parking her car in front of the house, she crossed the cracked sidewalk to mount the rickety steps. The wood gave noisily, as if it would break and send her tumbling through boards any minute. Stepping carefully, DeAndra moved quickly to avoid spending too much time on any step.

She rang the bell twice. The family-centered-sounds of the people within filtered out to her on the porch.

"I'll get it!" a woman's voice rang out over the sound of the television. The footsteps approaching the door were those of someone running. The sound of three separate locks sliding and rotating back reached her ears before the knob turned and someone wrenched the door open.

Sonia stood in the entryway, her short natural hair exposing all of her worn brown features. A hopeful, anticipatory look was on her face. That expression faded quickly when she saw that DeAndra was standing on the porch. "DeAndra," she said, a puzzled expression replacing the last and coloring her voice. "Evenin'."

"Hi Sonia. I dropped by to speak to Mouse for a minute." As if in explanation, DeAndra waved the little gift bag that held the gifts she'd brought back from Washington, D.C. Is she home?"

"No!" Sonia answered quickly, a curious note of regret in her voice as she turned her body to block most of the view of the area behind her. "Ah, she'd not here at the moment."

Staring at the space beyond Sonia's shoulder, DeAndra saw the moving tips of a pair of men's shoes, indicating that someone was standing just out of sight alongside the wall near the kitchen. She wondered if that was what Sonia did not want her to see. "Where is she?" she asked, hoping Sonia would be rattled enough to tell her the truth.

"She's…d-down south with her grandmother," Sonia stammered, visibly shaken. Fear filled her eyes and her hands trembled.

The sight of her frightened DeAndra and strengthened the conviction that something awful had happened. "Sonia, what's the matter?"

Sonia flinched. Her lips tightened and then flared out as if in anger.

A man in a dingy T-shirt and faded pants spoke from behind Sonia. "You again? You are one nosey bitch!"

"Eric!" Sonia told him not to talk to DeAndra that way and apologized for him.

Ignoring his sister, he continued. "Why don't you go home and mind your own business?"

DeAndra's gaze darted towards him, noting the black eye, swollen jaw, and split lip of Mouse's Uncle Eric. Someone had beaten the crap out of him. Could it be related to Mouse's disappearance? DeAndra wondered. "I was worried about Mouse when I didn't see her and someone told me that she ran away. If it's true, I want to help."

Startled, Sonia and her brother shared a quick look full of meaning.

"Somebody said she ran away? Who told you that?" the man snapped.

"Does it matter?" DeAndra countered calmly, determined not to let him intimidate her. "Is it true?"

He ignored her question and barked, "Sonia just told you where Mouse is. Are you calling her a liar?"

This time DeAndra ignored him, and turned to Sonia. "Sonia?"

"We don't need any help." Sonia's lips curved into a weak semblance of a smile, but a dark emotion still claimed her eyes. "When Mama gets back from church I'll call her. Mouse will call you later on."

Staring at her, DeAndra realized that for whatever reason, Sonia was hiding something that had to do with Mouse.

Sonia spoke again, the smile still on her lips. "Everything's fine, DeAndra. You'll be hearing from Michelle. Now, I've got something important to do, so I've got to go. Goodbye."

Sonia shut the door, but not before DeAndra caught the nasty smirk on Eric's battered face and saw the stiff way he moved. That beating hadn't improved his disposition one bit. He was still a nasty SOB. He disliked her personally with a disturbing virulence, and he didn't even know her. Shaking off all the negativity, she went down the steps and got into her car.

Satisfied that she'd done all she could for the moment, DeAndra went home and made an early dinner of macaroni and cheese, collard greens, and fried chicken. The food came out just right, but it was way too much for one person. Once she'd finished eating, she spent a lot time putting the food up in containers small enough for one person and stuffing most of them into the freezer.

Afterward, sitting at the cherry table in her brand new kitchen, an acute wave of loneliness hit her. Her thoughts slipped back to happier times, when she'd shared many meals with Damon. They'd laughed and talked about almost everything. He'd always been a good friend and a kind and caring person. There was no disputing that. Too bad his feelings had never grown to the kind of love she'd wanted and needed. Too bad for her that she couldn't forget about him.

Glancing at the clock sometime later, she turned her thoughts to Mouse. It was close to ten o'clock. Having made a point of being home all evening on the chance that the child would call, she felt disappointment. It was getting harder to ignore the growing conviction that she might never see the child again. There had to be something she could do.

After spending most of Monday morning in court playing catch up with her cases, DeAndra had lunch with her buddy, Bruce Moran, who was one of Chicago's finest. Like her, a large part of his day would be spent in court, but unlike DeAndra, he was testifying against some of the criminals he'd arrested.

Over submarine sandwiches and soda, she told him everything that had happened since she got back from Washington and confessed her fears and concerns about Mouse.

Bruce's sharp brown eyes pinned her in the smooth black leather booth where she sat. "Dee, don't go off on another crusade."

"What do you mean?" she asked, already knowing the answer. This was a conversation they'd had many times.

"I mean that you can't save the world. There's only one of you and billions of the rest of us and plenty of opportunities for everything to go wrong."

Ready to argue, she gritted her teeth as she finished her soda. "Right now, I'm only interested in saving one little girl."

"Who, by your own admission, may not need saving."

She nodded. That fact was indisputable, but she had a certain respect for her own gut instincts that had been proven over time. "Bruce, this isn't just a case of me having an overactive imagination. I know Sonia, and I know she was lying. I just can't figure out why. She loves her child. For her to be acting the way she was, something really bad has happened. Besides that, I'd be willing to bet that no one has seen Mouse in several days."

Bruce glanced at the bill and then reached into his pocket for cash. "Can you prove that? Can you prove that she's not with her grand-mother?"

Checking the bill, she laid a twenty on the table to cover her share of the bill and the tip. "I sure can try. Will you help me?"

"I'm kind of tied up right now with a case that's about to pop, but I want you to keep me up to date on this and I'll help you when I can. Where does her grandmother live anyway?"

"Somewhere in Alabama." Thinking back to some of the conversations she'd had with Mouse about her grandmother, the name of a town came to mind. "Cleary, Alabama."

"Is that anywhere near Birmingham?"

DeAndra shrugged. "I don't know. I'll look it up."

"It should be easy enough for me to find out," he said, turning as their server appeared at the table, checked the bill, and took what was due. Leaving tips on the table, DeAndra and Bruce left the restaurant and headed back to court.

DeAndra knew she had her work cut out for her. Unless she could prove that Sonia and Eric were lying or that there had been foul play, the police would stay out of it.

Driving home that night, she turned the problem of getting proof over in her mind. All her suspicions had started with Rico. Where did he fit in the puzzle? For that matter, where was he? When she'd taken Mouse home or driven through the neighborhood in the past, she'd usually seen Rico riding his bicycle. She now that she hadn't seen him since he rode by the center on Saturday.

On Tuesday, DeAndra spent most of her day in the office taking depositions and studying her files. Tomorrow she would be back in court. Even the weekly staff meeting, with the junior partner announcements, came as a welcome reprieve. Duly congratulating those who had been chosen, she went back to her office and the stack of files.

Weary at the end of the day, she left on time for a change. It took her twenty minutes to drive straight to Rico's house, which was a few blocks south of Mouse's.

Rico's grandmother, Rosa Valdez, was sitting on the porch in an old flowered housedress and a pair of flip-flops. Her silvery gray hair fell in looping waves that reached down past her shoulders. "Hey Chica, I know why you're here," she called as DeAndra came up the walkway and mounted the steps.

DeAndra smiled. "Okay Mrs. Valdez, why am I here?"

"You're stirring the neighborhood pot, and that's not a good thing. Everyone knows that you went to see the Browns yesterday and they're still upset."

"I only asked about Michelle," DeAndra said, feeling as if she had to defend herself, "I haven't seen her since I got back from Washington, and I'm worried. Rico told me that she ran away."

"That's true." Rosa nodded solemnly. "La niña did run away."

"Then why are the Brown's trying to convince me that she's down south with her grandmother?"

The older woman shot DeAndra a worried look. "I don't know. I don't like the atmosphere around here these days. That's why I sent Rico to stay with my brother for a while."

DeAndra dropped down in a spot next to the large pot of flowering plants. "You don't want me to talk to him?"

"No." Rosa's eyes were sympathetic but determined made her firm. "Let the niño be, DeAndra. She was his friend and I don't want him hurt, physically or mentally."

DeAndra bit her lip. "Does *anyone* know where Michelle is?"

"I doubt it." Rosa lifted a large blue plastic bowl into her lap and began to shell peas. "She's been gone for days."

Confounded, DeAndra gripped her bag in outrage. "And no one besides me is looking for her?"

"I didn't say that." Rosa glanced up briefly from her task to meet DeAndra's gaze. "Those two have talked to every child in the neighborhood and looked everywhere they could think of."

"You'd think they'd want the police in on the search," DeAndra muttered.

Something kin to fear flared briefly in Rosa's eyes. "Stay out of this one," she warned softly.

"You don't think…think she's dead?" DeAndra gasped.

"¡Madre de dios! I hope not." Rose set the bowl down, muttering softly to herself. "Sonia is okay, but that brother of hers-he's nothing but bad news."

DeAndra moved closer. "You know something about this, Rosa. Why don't you tell me? I won't tell anyone what you say…"

"I've said all I'm going to," Rosa said with conviction.

No matter how much DeAndra wheedled and begged, she refused to discuss the matter any further. Temporarily defeated, DeAndra thanked her and left for home.

She hadn't gone far when a loud, explosive sound split the air and something slammed into the right side of her windshield. Turning quickly, she saw a hole in the windshield and growing lines radiating out with an eerie cracking sound. Someone was shooting at her!

With a startled twist of her shoulders, DeAndra screamed. The car swerved to the left, veering over onto the wrong side of the street.

Passing within a dangerous inch of the parked cars, she hunkered down close to the steering wheel, her foot pressing hard on the accelerator as struggled to maintain control of the car.

Someone was shooting at her. Chilling fear crawled up her neck and spine, stiffening them and making her hands shake on the steering wheel. Her head whipped from side to side as she peered into the waning daylight, trying to see who was attacking her. The street was strangely empty. No witnesses, she thought, her head spinning wildly.

She pressed down harder on the accelerator, anxious to get out of the neighborhood and not caring if she got a ticket in the process. Hell, she thought, crazily laughing to herself, she would love to see one of Chicago's finest right about now.

She was still driving fast when she got on the Lakeshore Drive and sped in and out of the traffic. Still shaking, she pulled off at her exit, automatically driving to a place where she felt safe. Before she knew it, she was in the parking lot of Mort's, her favorite deli/liquor store, shutting off the engine. On shaky legs, she climbed out of the car and ran into the building.

The door slid open automatically. The owner stood near the counter. He looked up and took in her appearance. "Ms. Blake? Is everything okay?"

Words bubbled up, spilling out of her throat in an incoherent mess. "P-p-police! Call! Somebody!" She struggled to get an entire sentence out.

A knew but familiar voice sounded from the back of the store. "DeAndra? DeAndra! What's the matter? What's happened?"

She could only stare at the tall masculine figure in Dockers and an expensive blue golf shirt, her throat momentarily frozen with shock. He was the last person she expected to see in Chicago, her home turf.

CHAPTER EIGHT

In the store, Damon hurried towards her, concern for her welfare brimming in those deep green eyes. His strong arms opened and she ran into them, meeting him halfway.

"Damon!"

"It's all right, baby," he murmured gently. One hand smoothed damp wisps of hair away from her forehead. The other held her close, as if she were the most delicate, precious thing in the world. "You're okay now. You're safe with me."

DeAndra clung to him, her face on the soft cotton golf shirt covering his chest. The familiar scent of Damon and his cologne filled her nostrils and comforted her. He had been with her during some of the most memorable events in her life. It was fitting that he should be here to comfort her now. Concentrating on the loving comfort only he could give, she didn't question it.

When she had calmed, Damon urged her into a chair. Taking her hand, he gazed into her eyes and said, "DeAndra, tell me what happened so I can help you."

DeAndra stammered out the entire story, from seeing Rico at the center to visiting Rosa Valdez. She turned away when the tears started. Damon slung an arm around her shoulders and pressed Kleenex tissues into her hand. Then he had the storeowner call the police.

When the police officers arrived sometime later, Damon went out to the car with her, holding her hand in reassurance. Taking her key, he unlocked it and stood by while the police searched for evidence with their high-powered flashlights.

DeAndra's gaze kept returning to the ugly hole in the right side of the windshield and the stress lines radiating out from it. This was proof that someone seriously wanted to hurt her. *Kill*, she corrected herself. The distance between the hole in the passenger side and spot where she'd sat while driving the car was too close for comfort.

She forced herself to swallow. Her teeth were chattering.

Damon gathered her closer with an arm around her shoulders. "It won't be long now."

"A-ha!" One of the officers held up a pair of tweezers with small metallic object lodged between the prongs.

"I'd say twenty-two caliber," his partner said as he dropped it into a small plastic bag.

"If you're up to it, I can take a quick report right here and save you a trip to the station."

Agreeing quickly, she held on to Damon and followed the officers back to the patrol vehicle. Then she went through everything that had happened that day while the officer made notes on a pad.

"Hold up here a moment," the officer said, looking up from his pad. You were going around asking reluctant people questions about a missing child right before this incident happened?"

At DeAndra's affirmation he asked, "Why didn't you go to the police with this and let us do the investigating?"

"I did!" she protested. "At least informally." She repeated the conversation she'd had with Bruce. "He said I needed more proof that Mouse was missing."

"I'd say that with this incident, there's enough probable cause for the police to at least go and talk to this little girl's family," Damon observed.

Standing there, knowing that she could have been killed, she felt a small measure of relief that something positive would come out of this apparent attack on her life.

The officer quickly scanned the notes he'd made. "You're a lawyer. Have you received any threats related to your cases? Any disgruntled defendants and/or their families?"

DeAndra cleared her throat. "It's part of the job."

"Then give me some names and addresses to put on the report so they can be checked out," he ordered.

Her head spun. Having been in Mouse's neighborhood, and having been warned to stay out the situation with Mouse, she hadn't even considered that some of the people she'd encountered through her job could just as easily have shot through her window. She gave the officer several names and promised to call the station with the addresses as soon as possible.

"Where are you going to be so we can get in touch with you?" the officer asked when he'd completed his report. "I wouldn't advise you to go home tonight."

"You can stay with me," Damon offered, his hand tightening on hers.

Distanced from her emotions, a part of her chuckled at the irony of the situation. She'd spent an inordinate amount of time in her life trying to stay at Damon's place, and now that she'd moved away, here he was, voluntarily taking her in. "Thank you, Damon," she murmured in relief.

Only when she heard Damon give his name to the officer and a Chicago address that wasn't far from her condo did it hit her that something weird was going on. Damon lived in the Detroit area. What was he doing in Chicago with a Chicago address?

When she turned to stare at him, the words tumbled out. "I'll explain everything on the way home," he said, throwing her one of those "trust me" looks.

Mentally, DeAndra balked, but the look worked the way it always had. She would always trust Damon with everything but her heart. When she heard him verify that his name and address would not be released to the public or the press, she was really puzzled.

After the police were finished, Damon followed her to her favorite repair shop. Luckily, the manager was still there, closing things down for the night. As a favor to a faithful customer, he provided a spot in the repair area, so that the car could be repaired the next day. Handing over the keys, she climbed into Damon's yellow Mercedes-Benz SLK-class roadster convertible and settled herself on the charcoal leather seats.

Damon scanned her face. "Yes, I know. This is a little showy for me, but I love this car."

"I do too. It's a hot one." DeAndra pulled the seat belt around her and clicked it. Her fingers ran along the smooth, butter-soft leather on the seat and she inhaled the new car scent. Letting her head sink into the headrest, she asked, "Just what are you doing in Chicago?"

"Besides coming to your rescue?"

Ignoring the question, she kept looking at him, waiting until he answered.

"This isn't a permanent change. Believe it or not, I'm laying low for a while. Someone was writing me threatening letters and stalking me in Detroit. I went to Warfield with this about a month ago. When I got back from D.C., I found that they'd trashed my house."

"An old girlfriend?" she guessed, trying to glean an answer from his facial expression. His jaw was tight.

Checking his mirror, he changed lanes. "I doubt it. You know pretty much all my history, such as it is."

So he hadn't had a significant relationship since he'd been with her and Imani. Even now, she couldn't suppress the warm, expectant feeling that came over her. Would she ever get over her love for Damon?

"I don't know who this person is," he continued. "They're using a name that I've never seen before."

"They didn't hurt you?" DeAndra gasped, turning her body in the seat to face him.

Damon shook his head. "No, we didn't let it go that far, thank God. While I'm out of town, War has got some of his men working to figure out who it is." His brows wrinkled and his lips curled. "If you could have seen what they did to my house… I'm sure it was thousands of dollars worth of damage. The person that trashed my house is one sick individual. It'll never be the same for me again."

"You'd be surprised at what a good maid and some of these remodeling places can do," she began, intent on comforting him.

His voice was brisk, his tone resolute as he drove one-handed. "No. I'm going to sell it. I don't live there anymore."

She reached out and touched his other hand where it lay on the seat. He grasped her hand and squeezed. "Enough about me. You scared me back there in Mort's," he said. "You always have so much to say, but you could barely get your words out. And the way you ran in there... I thought someone was chasing you."

"I didn't know what to think," she said, emotion creeping back into her voice. She checked the passenger mirror, scanning the cars behind them.

"I'm ahead of you there," he assured her, "I've kept an eye on the traffic behind us. No one followed us to the garage and no one is following us now. You can relax."

"To tell you the truth, I don't know if I'll be able to relax until I know what happened to Mouse. For someone to try to kill me for asking questions…"

"For what it's worth, this incident does not have to be related to that child's disappearance, and I don't really think whoever shot at you was trying to kill you," he interrupted. "If they'd wanted to kill you, you'd be dead now. I think it was a warning for you to lay off the questions, at least for now. Are you going to?"

Biting her lip, DeAndra turned to look out the window. She wanted to give him her promise, but how could she? "I don't think I can. I never told you about all the scary things that happened all those years ago when I ran away.

"Mama worked two jobs and acted like a drill sergeant. We argued all the time and I was sick of the endless cycle of work and babysitting at home and the drudgery at school, so I saved my money and planned to run away. The first day was great. I hung out at the mall and window shopped till it got late. I'd already arranged to stay in my girlfriend's basement. By the second day, her parents knew I was there, so they called my mother. I ran before she got there."

DeAndra ran her the sides of her steepled fingers up and down the edge of her nose as she continued her story. "When it started getting late, I called all my friends, but none of their mothers would let me stay. Then I tried to spend the night in an empty abandoned house, three blocks over. A man in there grabbed me and exposed himself. I don't know how I managed to get away, but he chased me. Damon, he almost caught me."

"Did the police catch up with him?" Damon asked in a sympathetic voice.

DeAndra shook her head. "No. I kept running until I got to the all night drugstore. A group of boys saw me in there and threatened me. They'd taken my purse and the little money I had. They were trying to drag me out of the store when the manager threatened to call the police. When they arrived, I was never so glad to see the police. They took me home."

"How old were you?"

DeAndra hugged herself, the memory still fresh in her mind. "Twelve."

"That was some adventure for an twelve-year-old."

"Yes, and it's one I wouldn't want anyone to go through. I was one of the lucky ones. Damon, if she's still alive, something has to be done, fast."

"And that's why we have the police. This is something they're trained to do. Let them do their job." His voice turned sharp and commanding. "DeAndra, promise me that you will at least stay out of that neighborhood until the police have some answers."

The silence stretched on for several moments while she pretended to find the passing scenery of buildings, houses, and recreation areas interesting. She didn't like fighting with Damon. When she could stand it no more, she answered. "I'll try."

Damon's lips poked out as he concentrated on the road. She didn't need a crystal ball to know that he was angry and frustrated with her, but she wasn't going back down. She'd learned a long time ago that if you didn't stand up for what you believed in, you risked losing it. Stealing another glance at his profile, she realized that he had been one of the people who had taught her this.

"Did you get something to eat?" he asked after several minutes had passed.

"No. I'm not hungry." Her stomach still fluttered and ached from all the fear and excitement. Food was the last thing on her mind. Surprisingly, he pulled into the drive thru of a fast food restaurant and bought shakes, a burger, and a chef salad.

DeAndra wondered that he could eat so much and stay in such good shape. From what she could see, he was thinner than he'd been when she'd met him, years ago.

Damon headed for home. He drove his car up a driveway next to a beautiful, three-story greystone on a street filled with mansions that had been owned by some families for two or three generations. DeAndra's eyes widened when he parked the car in the garage out back.

"This belongs to Cotter," he explained, referring to his surgeon friend, Cotter Eastwood, as he got out of the car. Before he could come around to open her door, she was out, closing her door.

"I'm staying in his condo on the ground floor," he continued. "It has two bedrooms and two bathrooms, a large kitchen, living room, foyer, and deck. I'll give you the fifty-cent tour tomorrow. Come on in," he urged, closing the garage with the push of a button on his remote.

She followed him across the yard and up the steps. Above their heads, various lights warmed windows on each level. Anita Baker's voice wafted out into the night from an open window.

"Cotter rents the other units out," Damon explained, turning his key in the lock and pushing the door open. That's how he pays for this place. He just had it remodeled."

She stepped into a spacious foyer and stood on the patterned silk rug covering most of the hardwood floor. The fancy white chandelier hanging from the vaulted ceiling above her head commanded her attention with its gold accented wood ring that matched the floor. It created an optical illusion that made the white-walled room seem extra long.

Damon closed and locked the door. "I'll show you to your room, so you can get comfortable." He led her past the beige carpeted living room furnished with contemporary furniture, irregularly shaped couches and chairs in a mix of solids and prints.

Her room was decorated in a more traditional manner in a mix of rose, blue, and flax. It looked like something out of one of her dreams, from the floral fabric gathered into a ring high above to drape the big bed in mystery, to the soft blue carpet with small rose-colored squares. The cherrywood dresser stretched across the room with a large mirror that faced the bed.

"You'll be comfortable here," Damon said, ushering her into the room, "This is the room Cotter's sister Francine uses when she visits. She's about your size and her clothes will probably fit you." Pulling on a gold knob, he opened one of the dresser drawers to reveal a cavity overflowing with lingerie and sleepwear. His fingers snagged on a black lace thong and a matching strapless demi-bra.

Pretty sexy stuff for Cotter's snobby sister to be wearing, she observed, trying to classify the growing discomfort she felt watching Damon handle the lingerie.

Damon shoved the underwear aside, uncovering a transparent black silk negligee. Then he froze, as if suddenly realizing just what he was doing.

His gaze met hers and the sizzling heat in his eyes melted her insides and made her think about jumping his bones. She found herself reliving every glorious moment of the time she'd spent making love with Damon. No matter what she'd said or how she'd acted, wanting Damon had never been far from her mind.

One step forward and for the second time that evening she was enveloped in Damon's arms. This time she felt the sensitive tips of her breasts against the heat of his chest and the strength of his arms around her. She slipped one arm around his waist and stroked the soft hair at the nape of his neck with the other. "Damon," she whispered, tilting her head up to see his face and waiting for his kiss.

He traced one of her eyebrows with a fingertip that tailed down to her cheek. Leaning close, he followed the same path with his lips.

DeAndra's eyes drifted shut. His arms slid down her back and tightened around her. Suddenly, he released her. Her eyes opened wide with surprise.

"We can't do this right now," he muttered in a rusty voice. "You've had a shock and could have been killed. With all that's happened and where I am in my life, it wouldn't be right. I don't want to take advantage of you."

Balling her fists and squeezing her eyes shut, she counted to ten. When she was finished, she still saw him through a red haze of anger. "Don't presume to decide what's right for me!" she snapped, eyes sparking. "I'm not a child anymore and I know what I want. You can't tell me that you don't want it too."

Damon moved away from her, hurting her with his rejection. Pointing to the dresser and the closet to her left, he said, "Most of the stuff still has the tags on, so take what you need and don't worry about it." He turned away. "I'll be in the kitchen with my burger. The salad's yours if you want."

"No, but thank you." Her stomach still ached. Angry with herself, she didn't turn to look at him. She couldn't believe that she'd practically thrown herself at Damon and been rejected again. As soon as he exited the room, she shut the door and stretched out on the bed with her eyes closed. It had been a long, hard day.

Unlike most of the beds she experienced when she was away from home, this bed was soft and comfortable. With a hand to her throbbing forehead, she made her head comfortable on the pillow. Soon she fell asleep.

Damon went into the cavernous kitchen, placed the salad in the refrigerator and the extra shake in the freezer, and sat at the white resin and Formica table to have his burger and shake. He usually stayed away from fast food to keep his weight down, but it had gotten so late that he had given up all thoughts of cooking dinner for himself and DeAndra.

Unwrapping the sandwich, he bit into it and chewed. It was dry and had little flavor, but he continued to chew and swallow anyway. He still felt edgy from encountering a frightened DeAndra in the deli and knowing that she could have been killed. She was still frightened, yes, but stubborn and brave enough to put herself back in danger on the chance that she could save a little girl's life. Keeping her safe was going to be difficult.

Finishing the sandwich, he wiped his hands with a napkin and massaged the area between his eyebrows. He was frustrated for more than one reason. He'd always known that she was a very passionate woman, but never so much as the short time they'd been together. He'd been deeply in love with Imani, yes, but DeAndra had still been able to make him question the relationship when Imani began to realize that she still loved Perry.

Damon drank the strawberry shake. He was a man who tried to

stick to his convictions and usually succeeded. It had taken a lot for him to walk away from DeAndra a few minutes earlier. Despite his decision not to get involved romantically, he didn't know if he could do it again.

CHAPTER NINE

Although DeAndra slept deeply, it was only for two to three hours at a time. Each time she would awaken in the unfamiliar bed to the strange, padded silence of the guest room. During one of those intervals, she removed her clothes and used the bathroom to shower, wash her underwear, and get ready for bed. Rather than sleep nude, she tore the tags off an elegant beige silk nightgown with lace covering the bodice and a split up one side. Slipping on the gown and tossing the matching robe on the foot of the bed, she climbed between the sheets.

When she woke up for the fourth time and the clock showed only five o'clock, she sat up in bed and watched the darkness turn to light at the center of the drapes. Donning the robe, she left the room and went in search of the kitchen. Moving from room to room as quietly as possible, she found the master suite where Damon still slept peacefully, a fully equipped exercise room, first floor laundry, and a gorgeous office filled with contemporary furniture.

In the kitchen at last, she examined the cabinets until she found the built in Sub-Zero refrigerator/freezer. Opening it, she discovered that it was full of food. Her stomach growled noisily and she laughed inwardly, glad there was no one to hear. She hadn't consciously known that she was hungry.

Finding eggs, honey ham, green onions, cheddar cheese, and margarine, she decided to make omelets. Placing the ingredients on the counter, she chopped vegetables, ham and cheese. In one of the cupboards, she found Starbucks coffee and started it in the coffee maker. Then she searched for an omelet pan.

Damon rolled over in bed sniffing, the air. Was that coffee he smelled? A while ago he thought he'd heard the door to his room open, but when he'd pried his eyes open, there'd been no one there. He told himself that if DeAndra had made her way to his room, she would be in bed with him now. Though he knew that the last thing he needed right now was to get deeply involved with her again, he could not quell the disappointment that lingered in his thoughts.

Sniffing the air once more, Damon sat up. He definitely smelled coffee, and eggs and ham too. DeAndra was cooking in the kitchen. His imagination went into overdrive. In a flash he was out of the bed and into the bathroom. Within moments he stepped into a cold shower. *Maybe this will cool my jets*, he mused.

By the time he'd showered and dressed, the smell of food was stronger, and his mouth was watering. The door to his room was ajar, leading him to believe that DeAndra had already called him for breakfast. Feeling refreshed, he went for the kitchen.

In a beige silk negligee and robe that showcased all her physical assets and hid very little, DeAndra stood by the table, pouring coffee. Damon nearly choked, his gaze going for the lace barely covering her lush breasts and the smooth lines where the gown caressed her small waist and the luscious curve of her butt. She looked hot and sensual, and ready to spend the day in bed making love. Fleetingly he wondered if she was trying to punish him for walking away from her last night.

"Good morning." Her gaze met his briefly and she turned to add cream to both mugs of coffee.

"Good morning," he managed, his voice only a little hoarse.

"I tried to call you for breakfast, but you were in the shower," she said inanely, apparently unaware of her effect on him.

"No harm done," he answered, moving to the table filled with plates, silverware, mugs, and food that looked like something out of a cookbook. Drawing a chair back, he sat down, glad to be able to hide a growing erection. He was ashamed of himself. It wasn't as if he were a youth, unable to control his body. He was a grown man who couldn't remember the last time something like this had happened to him.

While she took the seat across from him, he began to do the multiplication tables in his head, backwards. That seemed to help. He'd gotten through two sets when he noticed that the room was utterly silent. Steeling himself, he glanced at her.

"I *can* cook," she said, giving him a puzzled look. "Aren't you going to eat?"

"Of course. And thanks for cooking breakfast."

"With you taking me in like this, it was the least I could do," she said.

"You are and always will be welcome in my house, DeAndra, no question." He made a show of adding sugar to his coffee. "I was just...getting my head together."

She chuckled. "After all these years, I know you're not a morning person."

Stirring the coffee, he put the spoon down, took a long sip of the mixture and swallowed. Replacing the cup, he decided that he felt better already. "You're not going in to work today, are you?" he asked, lifting his knife and fork and cutting into his ham and cheese omelet."

Her voice was soft and precise. "No, I think I'd better call in until I hear something more from the police. You don't think I should go in?"

He put flavor-filled chunks of the omelet into his mouth and chewed, savoring the taste. The food was delicious. Then realizing that she was waiting for his response, he gave her another quick glance, careful to focus only on her anxious face. "Of course not," he reassured her.

She sighed with relief. "Good. I actually have a lot of my work in my briefcase, so I can work here today with no problem."

Good. Damon sighed inwardly. That meant that she would probably spend most of the day in Cotter's office, out of sight and out of mind. He finished his breakfast with gusto.

"Damon, what's going on? Are you angry with me about something? You've barely looked me in the face this morning." The anxiousness was back in her voice.

Slowly lifting his head, he stared straight into her big brown eyes. Unfortunately, after a moment or two, his gaze dropped, to take in her lace-covered breasts, where the chocolate-colored tips were identifiable beneath the nearly sheer covering. His mouth watered, this time for an entirely different reason. He tried to force his gaze upward, but this time, his brain wasn't listening. Beneath his scrutiny, the tips of her breasts hardened into nubs that stood out easily.

"Oh!" DeAndra looked down at her breasts and then back at Damon. She crossed her arms in front of them. "I-I wasn't trying to—to…"

"I know," he reassured her, the hoarseness creeping back into his voice.

Arms still folded in front of her breasts, she stood up, poised to rush back to her room. Then she made the mistake of looking down, and saw just how much of her body the thin silk gown and robe revealed. She sat down again in a hurry. "I might as well be standing here naked!" she mused.

"*I know.*" Damon cleared his throat, already back to work on the multiplication tables.

She rubbed a hand over her eyes. "Damon, I'm sorry. Believe it or not, this was the most conservative sleepwear I could find in that room."

"I believe you. Francine obviously uses this place to meet her boyfriends away from the beady eyes of her family." He reached across the table to grasp her hand. "DeAndra, I'd be lying if I said I didn't enjoy the view. You have a beautiful body, one that could generate enough fantasies to last a lifetime."

Her hand clasped his, realization dawning on her face. "Oh, Damon," she murmured, "I don't want to make you uncomfortable. Besides, when you keep staring at me like that, my mind goes places it definitely shouldn't." Scanning his face, her eyes widened and she pulled her hand from his. "Okay, now stop. You're making me hot!" She folded her arms in front of her, obscuring his view of her gorgeous breasts.

"Is that such a bad thing?" Damon barely recognized his own voice. He wasn't just asking DeAndra; he was asking himself. His body had had about enough of him being noble. Would it be so bad if he and DeAndra took at turn at burning the sheets?

DeAndra nodded in answer to his question. "For me, yes. You were right last night. I can't be with you like I was before. It means something different to you. I know that people get hot and bothered and sleep together all the time, but that has never been who I am."

"No, it hasn't." This time he had no trouble keeping his gaze on her face. He saw the sincerity in her eyes and heard the determination in her voice. He didn't know how long he and DeAndra would be sharing this place, but he hoped she had enough determination for the both of them.

Damon gazed deep into his coffee cup. "Go put something on," he ordered. He didn't look up when she got up from the table. He didn't have to. The enticing vision of DeAndra in that thin silk was imprinted on his brain.

Damon finished his coffee. He cleared and washed the stove and table. Then he rinsed the dirty dishes and put them in the dishwasher. When DeAndra failed to return, he decided that she'd probably changed and then gone to work in Cotter's office.

He thought about the things he'd planned to do before he'd run into DeAndra. The list included a walk along the Navy Pier, a trip to the Magnificent Mile to buy slacks and shirts, and a stop at the park to see if there was live music. Theoretically, he could still do those things while she did her casework, but could he trust her to stay in the condo, where it was safe? Damon sighed. He couldn't take the chance.

Damon carefully peered into Cotter's office to find DeAndra on the phone. She had changed back into the teal suit she'd been wearing yesterday, but her feet were bare. Thankfully, the suit covered everything but her long shapely legs. Damon tore his gaze away from them.

"I'll be working outside the office today," she said, speaking into the telephone. "And tomorrow I'll be in court all day. If you need me for anything or one of the clients has a question, you can reach me on my cell phone or the number I just gave you. What?" Her mouth turned up at the corners and she chuckled as one of her ruby–painted toenails moved back and forth through the plush aqua carpeting. "No, this is not about a man. Celia, why does every change in my routine have to be about a man?"

DeAndra listened quietly for a few moments and then she burst into laughter. "Okay, Celia, I'll check in with you tomorrow. Bye."

Replacing the phone, she saw Damon standing in the doorway. "I didn't want to tell them that someone shot at me," she said.

He nodded. "I can understand that. Hopefully the police will come through in the next couple of days." Shifting his feet, he changed the subject. "I see you changed clothes."

"Yeah. Is this better?" she asked, tugging at the short slim skirt of her suit.

"Yes, but it's a bit formal, don't you think?"

"I don't think I have much of a choice otherwise. If you can do better, go ahead. Check out Francine's closet. The choices are Victoria's Secret type clothing or spandex."

Damon tossed her a doubtful look and rubbed his fingers across his clean-shaven chin. Because he'd decided to behave himself and meant to stick to it, he didn't want DeAndra walking around his place with all her physical assets on display. "I vote for a two to three hours' casework and then we go down to the Magnificent Mile to get you a few things to wear and the Navy Pier afterward if we're not too tired."

DeAndra shook her head. Her fingers zeroed in on the shorter hair on top, and plucked and fluffed in her trademark nervous gesture. "No, I just got my condo and I've been spending a lot of money on furniture and window treatments. I can't afford to buy any more clothes right now."

He blew out his breath in a rude rumble. "That should be the least of your worries. I've got good plastic and cash. We could get a few things to tide you over."

"I don't know when I'll be able to pay you back."

"And I won't ask you to," he said smartly.

"Damon, I'm not some kid you're mentoring anymore. I'm a grown woman who makes good money and I can pay my own way."

Damon saluted her. "Yes, ma'am. Now that that's settled, I've got some work to do. I'll meet you at the door in a couple of hours."

Moving her arms and touching the teal fabric, she examined her suit. He'd already noticed that it wasn't as fresh as it once was. Finally she shrugged and agreed in a resigned voice, "Okay, Damon. You don't think I should be worried about being out shopping in public?"

"Of course not. If someone really is after you, they'll be watching your place and your office, and maybe the court. Who'd be looking for you on the Miracle Mile or Navy Pier?"

She shrugged in answer. "See you in three hours."

Going to his room, Damon dug out his briefcase. He was quite pleased with himself at having managed to find a way to visit the Magnificent Mile and Navy Pier as he'd originally planned, while keeping DeAndra safely in view.

Thinking about his own troubled situation with the stalker in Detroit, he called Clay for a status report. "So what's going on with the situation at home? Any news?" he asked after dispensing with the pleasantries.

"Nothing definite enough to make an arrest tomorrow, but things are moving along. Dennis has been out twice impersonating you. The only problem has been that there are several people who have been around each time and no one has done anything that raises a flag. We've got the prints we lifted back from the lab and they don't match any in all the files we've accessed, local, state, or federal. A lot of people have been trying to dig your whereabouts out of your secretary. I've given her the secret Caribbean vacation story and insisted that she tell it to everyone, including her best buddy, Candy."

Damon scribbled on a pad. "Sounds like you guys have been busy."

With a tired sigh, Clay responded. "Yes, Damon, we have. I hope you're not getting restless already. Just chill, ol' buddy. This could be your life we're talking about."

"Listen, ol' man. You're the one who needs to chill. I know how important this is. I'm okay for now. I just called for a status report. Is that too much for the victim to ask?"

He heard Clay laughing on the other end. "So how've you been keeping busy?"

"I was planning to do a lot of the touristy things when I ran into DeAndra…"

"Wheee-oooh!" Clay's response was so loud that Damon pulled the phone away from his ear. "Now that was one hot little number and it only burned for you! If you didn't get into those panties, something is wrong with you!"

"I'm not going there, and neither should you," Damon admonished him. "Someone shot into her car yesterday and frightened the daylights out of her."

"This has got to an all-time kicker. I send you off to lay low and you hook up with someone who's being shot at. I can't help you on this one 'cause it's out of my jurisdiction."

"CPD is on this one," Damon assured him. "A little girl who helps out at a legal aid center is missing and it seems that DeAndra has been asking too many questions."

"Well, Damon, I'd advise you to stay away from reporters, camera men, and anyone who might recognize you. You and DeAndra should lay low, if you aren't doing that already, that is!" Devilish laughter broke out on the other end of the phone once more.

"Now that I've brought you your humor for the day, I've got some work to do," Damon said in a tone that made it clear that he thought his current situation was anything but funny.

Clay ignored Damon's dry tone. "Okay, buddy, we'll keep you posted."

Replacing the receiver, Damon retrieved his case from a corner of the room. Opening it, he drew out written briefs from the lawyers in a case he'd heard two weeks ago. He had another month before he had to render his decision, but he was one to ponder his cases long and hard in the name of justice. Taking the briefs, he settled into the recliner next to the bed and adjusted the lamp. Then he began to read, engrossing himself in the material. Hours later, at the musical sound of DeAndra's voice, he looked up in surprise.

"I've been waiting for you in the living room for a good fifteen minutes. Did you change your mind about going out?"

"No." He checked his watch to see that three hours and fifteen minutes had passed. "I was so deep into this case that I forgot the time."

"You really love your work and you're good at it. That's one of things I've always admired about you," she said, coming closer.

Thanking her for the compliment, he smiled, aware that in the past she would have pulled up a chair to quiz him about the case. He blamed himself for the guarded affection he saw in her eyes.

Damon put the briefs back into the files and locked them in his briefcase. Checking his wallet, he stood. "I'm ready if you are."

"Are we driving, or were you planning to take the train?"

"I've never been on one of Chicago's trains, so I thought I'd try it. Do you mind?"

"No. This could be an adventure for us." DeAndra grabbed her purse and followed him out.

Damon enjoyed the adventure of deciding which line they would take and purchasing the cards at the station. DeAndra walked close to him and talked about her firm while they waited for the train. From her conversation, he gathered that she worked hard and was paid accordingly, but that the firm had been slow to make any sort of commitment to her. The commitment DeAndra wanted was entry into the coveted junior partner program.

He tried to give her some perspective by telling her that her current problem was one that every young lawyer faced. Because she was a good lawyer, her firm would not be able to stay noncommittal in regard to her future. As she gained experience and her reputation grew, other firms would offer her more permanent arrangements.

Shopping on the Magnificent Mile with DeAndra, Damon felt their years apart melt away as the old camaraderie came back. They strolled down Michigan Avenue with the crowds of tourists and workers, going in and out of the stores. DeAndra selected outfits, modeled them for him, and even considered his opinions in her selections.

They went into Lord and Taylor's, where Damon stayed in the background while she purchased lingerie, a conservative blue cotton gown, and a cotton terry robe, but helped her select a soft, multicolored top and casual slacks.

In Marshall Fields, Damon talked her into buying a lemon yellow suit that draped her neckline and was accented with fancy navy-blue buttons. On a high from shopping, she also bought a yellow pair of Ferragamo sling backs and a comfortable pair of walking shoes.

DeAndra changed into her most comfortable new clothing in the ladies' room while Damon arranged for the packages to be delivered to the house. Then they jumped into a cab and headed for the Navy Pier.

They stepped onto the sidewalk outside the pier and walked through the gates with several small groups of different ethnic people. Damon looked around, enjoying the carnival like atmosphere. Various vendors lined the pier, selling popcorn, cotton candy, ice cream, and souvenirs. There was even a mall for browsing away from the sun, and a funhouse reminiscent of the old amusement parks Damon had visited as a boy.

After they strolled all the way down to the Ferris wheel, DeAndra insisted on a ride. Way up high, the couple looked out on several of the boats for hire in the locks and those gliding gracefully on the lake. One big, yellow boat was speeding around the lake, water kicking up in its wake. He pointed to it. "I want to ride that one."

She laughed. "I didn't know you were so adventuresome."

"There's a lot you don't know about me," he said, holding onto the railing as they traveled high into the air. "A man can change a lot in two years."

"Not the person deep inside," she insisted.

Their gazes locked, each certain they were right, neither ready to back down. Finally, as if by agreement, they both let their attention wander as the wheel took them down to the ground.

CHAPTER TEN

The phone was ringing when Damon and DeAndra arrived at his place. He quickly locked the front door. When he answered, DeAndra stood near and heard an authoritative male voice asking for her.

With raised eyebrows, Damon gave her the phone. Lifting the phone to her ear, she spoke into the receiver. When her name was repeated, she recognized the voice. "Bruce! How'd you find me here?"

Surprised to hear his voice, she was more surprised to hear that he'd seen her file at the station and volunteered to take it on. When he asked where she'd been, she gave him the highlights of their day. She chattered on until she noticed that Bruce was unusually silent. Then she used what she knew of his personality to interpret it. "You've found something already, haven't you?" she asked.

"Yeah." He managed to infuse a smile of satisfaction into his tone. "I went and had a talk with Sonia this morning. She was kind of cagey, but finally admitted that her daughter is missing."

DeAndra felt triumphant that her instincts had been right, but the fear that had been festering in the back of her thoughts grew. Her fingers strangled the phone. "Since when?"

"Since the day before you got back from Washington. Apparently, her uncle tried to punish her for something and got carried away. He beat her pretty badly, according to Sonia."

"I was afraid of that," she gasped, thinking back to when she'd stood on Sonia's porch and felt pure meanness emanating from Mouse's uncle.

"Sonia was so upset that she called the child's father and he beat the crap out of her brother. They were afraid to take the child for medical treatment for fear she would be taken away from them and the uncle would be sent to jail. Sonia works two jobs and even with the wages her brother gets for working as a janitor, they're barely making it."

Thinking about poor Mouse and what it must have been like for her, DeAndra's eyes stung with tears. She knew what it was like to be helpless with someone bigger preying on you, abusing you. She'd experienced that as a child too when a bully had pestered, beaten, and harassed her for weeks, and her mother had not been around to protect her either. "So where is Mouse?"

"They don't know. They've been out looking for her every day. Sonia's been at her wit's end."

"Yeah, so much that she lied when I tried to help her," DeAndra put in angrily.

"You can understand why she did what she did...," Bruce began.

"But I can't condone it," she insisted. "There're just too many crazy people out there." She felt the comforting weight of Damon's hand on her shoulder.

"Given the circumstances, we looked around the place. I hope not, but Sonia's daughter could very well be dead."

"I thought of that too," she sighed, swallowing hard and clamping down on her imagination.

"The reason I'm telling you this is because we found something. There was a 22 caliber pistol stuffed in a hole beneath the house."

"No." DeAndra dragged a hand across her right eye. She felt a little shaky. She wondered if Sonia and her brother had tried to kill her. She couldn't let herself believe that because that would also mean that Mouse was dead.

"Sonia and her brother both claimed that they didn't know it was there. We took the gun in for prints and ballistic tests. My gut tells me that it's the gun that was used to shoot into your car. Until we know for sure, stay where you are."

"What about court tomorrow?" she asked, remembering that she had cases to represent in court in the morning. "I have to be there."

"That should be okay, but be careful."

Swallowing past the lump in her throat, she wiped away the one tear that had managed to fall. "Okay, Bruce. I really appreciate your sharing the information with me."

"Just keep it to yourself."

Her voice rose higher than normal. "But I have to tell Damon. He's the friend I'm staying with and he's a judge in Michigan."

"I guess it'll be okay, but no one else."

"Thanks again," she murmured.

"Dee, I can tell you're upset. Do you want me to come over there?" Bruce offered.

"No, Damon's here. I'll be all right."

"I'll be home if you change your mind," Bruce added. Then they said their goodbyes and hung up the phone.

"Damon," she said, ready to launch into an explanation.

"I've already heard most of it," he said, opening his arms to embrace her once more. His lips brushed her temple in a gesture that somehow seemed less innocent than it had in the past.

I could get used to this. She rested her head against his chest, her teeth fumbling with her bottom lip as she held onto his solid warmth.

Damon's voice was low and soothing. "DeAndra, it's going to be all right. It really is. They'll find her and we'll help."

Determined to do what she could, she considered how she might find Rico and remembered the Samba Grill, a little South American restaurant that was close to the neighborhood where Rosa's brother stayed. She suggested they have dinner there, hoping they might get lucky and spot Rico somewhere nearby.

With its Caribbean-Latin menu, the little restaurant was so popular that they had to wait in a long line of eager customers. Finally seated, they pored over the exciting menu, not sure what to order. Finally, DeAndra settled on *fricassee de pollo*, which was chicken breast marinated in lime juice, garlic, and cumin, then roasted in a stew with onions, peppers, bacon, cilantro, carrots, potatoes, and white wine. Damon chose *filete de palomilla*, grilled filet mignon with sautéed red onions and jalapeño garlic mashed potatoes. The food was spicy and delicious. Sampling each other's plates, the couple savored each heavenly bite. Afterward, too full for dessert, they paid the bill and strolled back to the car.

Turning into the neighborhood at the corner, Damon drove up the street. Belatedly, DeAndra thought about the expensive yellow car and how conspicuous it was. As they drove up and down several streets of the area, they stood out, collecting attention like a mouse in a yard full of cats.

She was close to giving up when she spotted a familiar figure ahead of them in an orange, rust, and yellow-stripped shirt and worn blue jeans. He was riding his bicycle in the street. Rolling down the window, she called to him. "Rico!"

He turned to look at them, a startled expression on his face that quickly transitioned to surprise and then pleasure. Braking, he climbed off the seat and waited for them to catch up. "Hi Ms. Blake. Is everything okay?"

Noting the element of genuine concern in his voice, she ignored the questions in her mind and smiled. "Hi Rico. Everything's fine."

The child scanned her for a few moments, as if satisfying himself that her statement was true, and then his attention shifted to Damon's car. "A Benz! Hey, this car is slamming!" He moved closer, admiration sparkling in his eyes as he caressed the car with his gaze, from the 18-inch AMG wheels to the retractable hardtop.

When his perusal reached Damon behind the wheel, Rico turned to DeAndra. "Is that your new boyfriend?"

She shared a quick glance with Damon. Damon obviously found the boy and his question amusing. "That's none of your business, Rico," she answered with enough bite for him to get the point. "This is my friend, Damon Kessler."

"How do you do, sir?" the boy asked politely. "I am Rodrico Valdez, but everyone calls me Rico." He extended a hand into the car.

Damon shook it solemnly. "Nice to meet you, Rico."

"Where've you been, Rico?" she began carefully. "I haven't seen you in a while."

He nodded. "That's because my grandmother made me come and stay with Uncle Antonio. She said that things were getting too hot after Chelle ran away."

"I'm sure she was trying to keep you safe, Rico," she said, suddenly aware and ashamed that she could be putting the child in danger just by talking to him. "Just tell me where Mouse went. Her mother and her uncle have already told the police that she ran away."

When he hesitated, she prompted him. "Come on, Rico. I won't tell anyone who told me."

His brows furrowed. "She's not there anymore."

DeAndra studied him. "How do you know?"

"Because I checked just before my grandmother made me come here."

"Just tell me where the place is so we can go and see for ourselves."

Shadows crept into the child's eyes. "It's in the neighborhood."

DeAndra's eyes widened in surprise. "Someone told you about what happened to my car," she stammered, mentally distancing herself from what had happened.

"They shot at you, Ms. Blake. I don't want you to get hurt."

"I can take care of myself," she insisted, ignoring the frightened voice in her head. Damon's hand covered hers with comforting warmth. She paused. "Rico…"

Rico leaned into the car, concerns too weighty for a child still flickering in his eyes. "It's the boarded-up house on the corner of Velago and Rio. If you go around the back, you can lift the board covering the back door and go in. Be careful, Ms. Blake…"

"Thanks, Rico, I'll be careful," she answered.

"We should probably call the police on this one," Damon said as soon as they'd driven off.

"And tell them what?" she asked, remembering her promise to Rico.

Damon didn't answer. He drove in silence for several miles.

Checking the scenery outside the car, she turned to him with a new realization. "Damon, you're headed back to your place. I thought you were going to help me look for Mouse."

He tossed her an incredulous look. "We can't go in this car."

She had to agree with him. Damon's car was one that would be noticed, wherever he went. "What are you going to do?"

"Borrow the car Cotter's grandmother used to drive. He got so attached to it after she died that he couldn't sell it. It's a lot less conspicuous than this one."

At the house, he put the yellow convertible in the garage and backed out a black Honda Accord that looked almost new.

"The keys were in the glove box," he explained as she climbed in and settled on the soft leather seats. "I'll be right back," he said, getting out of the car and jogging into the house.

When he returned, he'd changed the tan cotton knit for a loose, button-down black shirt. DeAndra scanned him in confusion. Why had he changed? Then it hit her. She stared at the shirt, trying to see through it as he backed out of the driveway. "Damon, are you carrying a gun?"

"Yes." He didn't miss a beat. "I got a permit to carry it when my life was threatened a while back. I wouldn't go sneaking around without one."

She couldn't take her eyes off him. Her mouth moved uselessly, not voicing any of the questions running through her head. One thing for certain, Damon had changed his position on guns. Until now, he'd hated them and refused to carry one.

"You don't you think you'll have to use it?" she asked, feeling silly for asking, but needing to hear the answer.

"Let's hope not." Clearing the driveway, he straightened the car and drove off. DeAndra opened her purse to search for the small can of mace that she carried but had never had an occasion to use.

It was nearly dark by the time they made it to the abandoned house. Scanning the block of houses and surrounding cars, DeAndra felt vulnerable. Her heart was beating so fast that she could barely catch her breath and her hands were cold.

It was bad enough to think that Sonia and her brother had shot at her, but what if it had been someone else and they were here, waiting to finish the job? She clenched her jaw and remembered something Damon had told her long ago: "The truly important things that must be done in this world are not easy and most of the time, they're thankless jobs, but without the real heroes of our time, humanity would be lost. Stand by your convictions."

Damon spoke from his side of the car. "DeAndra, do you want to change your mind? It's okay if you do. There's no telling what we'll see in this place and this isn't the smartest thing we could do. We probably should have asked your friend Bruce to come along."

She shook her head. "No. He'd have wanted to talk to Rico and I can't have that. I just want to make sure she's not there, and see if there's anything to prove that she was, anything to prove that she might still be alive. I still want to go in, Damon."

He sighed, reaching for his door. "All right then, let's get it over with."

Thankfully, no one was out and about when they got out the car and crossed the broken concrete to go around the dark, dilapidated structure to the back. No one in the neighboring homes pulled aside their curtains or shades to look. The rowdy sounds of children outside playing on the next block filled the air.

DeAndra hated the loud creaking sound the door made once they'd lifted the wooden bars to clear the battered back door. Despite her flashlight, she hated going into the dark house. It was like stepping into a gloomy hole, full of the unknown and brought back too many memories of the past. She felt as if she couldn't breathe. Then she realized that she was holding her breath. Forcing a breath and switching on her flashlight, she slowly followed Damon inside.

With almost synchronized dance of light, they flashed their lights around the house to make sure no one hid in the shadows. The kitchen was an empty room with peeling tile covered with grime. The walls were stained with dirt, grease, and life. People had lived in this place and called it home. She kept her flashlight trained mostly on the floor as they trekked from room to room, finding nothing but trash and filth.

By unspoken agreement, they mounted the stairs, holding on to the shaky railing. A large hole in the floor marked their arrival at the top. Adrenalin shot through her as she surveyed it and the area around it. "There's room," Damon called to her. Edging around it with her close behind, he stepped carefully into one of the bedrooms and hit they pay dirt.

An old battered mattress was on the floor in a corner. Someone had covered most of it with an old gold curtain. She shined the light on it, certain that the brown stains it sported were dried blood. Forcing a swallow past the lump in her throat, she bit her lip as her light shined on an old lantern and a book of matches. "She was here."

"It could have been anyone," Damon cautioned. "There's nothing here to prove it was your friend."

Something bright and yellow gleamed in the light, near one end of the mattress. She picked it up and examined it, a feeling of triumph clamping down on the fear she'd been fighting ever since she'd come into the house. "Yes, there is." Turning the object so that he could read the name engraved upon it, DeAndra continued, "I gave her this pen for her birthday."

The heavy slam of something falling on the stairs, followed by several fumbling noises, interrupted them. With a squeak that would have done a mouse proud, DeAndra nearly jumped out of her skin.

Cursing under his breath, Damon searched for a place to hide. "Come on!" He pushed towards the only possibility, the tiny closet with the remains of a French door half on, half off the track.

Scooting in, she drew a quick breath while Damon crammed himself in behind her and adjusted the door to cover them. Her hips were tight against his crotch and his chest was against her back. DeAndra felt a new kind of excitement strumming through her veins, making it hard for her to concentrate.

Cursing her raging hormones, she tried to maneuver her body to put some space between them, and bumped her hip against the hard edge of the wall. Sharp pain reverberated through her as she bit back a cry.

"Don't move!" Damon hissed in a strangled voice.

She felt him fumbling with his shirt and guessed that he was retrieving the gun. Against her back, his heart hammered in the darkness, just as fast as hers did. The combined sounds of their breathing filled her ears, dangerously loud.

Footsteps sounded in the room. Through the place where the door was off the track and between the slats, she saw a flashlight dancing off the walls.

Trembling, she wished she were the one holding the gun. Damon could be trusted to keep both of them from getting hurt, but she hated the helpless feeling stealing over her. It was only a matter of time before whoever it was opened the closet and discovered them.

With as much stealth as she could muster, DeAndra searched her purse for the can of mace.

The footsteps in the room halted right outside the closet. "Ms. Blake?" a man's voice called. "I know you and your friend are in there. This is Mitch Wright, Michelle's dad. I followed you two in here. I just want to talk to you. Will you come out?"

"We've got a gun," Damon warned in a voice that left no doubt that he was prepared to use it.

"You won't need it," the other man said quickly. "Please, I'm just hoping you two found something. I've been searching for days and I haven't found a thing."

Damon pushed the closet door open, the gun still in his hand. "You took a big chance sneaking up on us like that."

Standing in front of the closet, Mitch's dark-circled eyes held a desperate look. "Hey man, I'm sorry. I didn't mean anything by it. I've been combing the neighborhood every night, so when I saw an unfamiliar car, I followed at a distance. I saw Ms. Blake getting out of the car and coming back here with you. I know how crazy Michelle is about Ms. Blake, so I followed, hoping that Michelle would show up."

It was scary to think that someone had been following them and they hadn't even noticed. *You never claimed to be anything but an amateur*, DeAndra reminded herself as she stepped out of the closet and made quick introductions. "I'm sorry, Mitch, but I don't know where she is."

Mitch's head dropped in disappointment. "Did you find anything?" he asked in a voice with no aspiration of hope.

"Just the pen I gave her for her birthday." She held it up in the beam of the flashlight.

"So she was here." Mitch went back to looking around the room, his gaze falling on the thin mattress. "Anything could have happened here."

"Exactly." Damon stuffed the gun back under his shirt.

Mitch shook the curtain that covered the mattress and looked beneath it. "What made you check this place?"

"Just a hunch. I know everyone checked all the open places," she said, determined to keep her promise to Rico. "This one seemed boarded up and locked, but it wasn't."

"We're leaving," Damon said. "There's nothing here."

"So what's next?" Mitch asked, his voice filled with frustration.

"We turn the pen and information about this abandoned house over to the police," Damon told him.

DeAndra called her friend Bruce, and he met them at Damon's to take down the information. He was a bit angry with her for going back into the neighborhood and putting herself in further danger, but he was also glad to get a new lead on Michelle's disappearance. He pressed her about the information she'd gotten that had caused her to search the house and sensed that she was withholding something. Finally, giving her a hug as he prepared to leave, he said, "Don't go home or back into that neighborhood until we're certain about the gun and can ID the perpetrator."

When DeAndra nodded obediently, Bruce turned to Damon. "DeAndra sometimes gets herself confused with superwoman, only she's a lot more impulsive. I'm looking to you to help her resist any further urges to put herself in danger."

"I'll do my best," Damon said.

Once Bruce left, DeAndra retired to the guest room, wound up but tired from all that she'd done and experienced during the day. She wasn't used to so much adventure in her life. A new hopefulness filled her as she said a prayer for Mouse.

She wasn't used to being around Damon so much, either. Tall, handsome, caring, and brilliant, he was everything she'd ever wanted in a man. How could she have forgotten how the excitement simmered within her, always close to the surface, just from being around him? When they'd been hiding in the closet, she'd even imagined that he'd begun to harden beneath the press of her hips. She wanted Damon and there was no getting around it.

Stripping quickly, she crossed the plush carpeting to enter the bathroom. She stepped into a cool shower and kept it that way, anything to put a lid on her libido. Afterward, she dried herself and could not resist putting on the tiny black string bikini that she'd added to her clothing purchases when Damon had gone to get a cup of coffee.

Staring at herself in the mirror, she imagined herself seducing Damon. She'd done it before. It could be done again. But what would it mean? Did it have to mean anything besides the fact that she would get her rocks off by sleeping with the only man she'd ever loved?

Walking back into the bedroom, DeAndra looked at the modest, blue cotton gown that she'd also purchased. That was what she should be wearing. It didn't matter, she finally decided as she drew back the covers, climbed into the bed, and got comfortable on the satin sheets. Damon wasn't going to see her in it.

After a useless hour of lying in bed and staring up at the ceiling in the dark, she turned on the light and glanced around the room. A few books on the dresser caught her attention. Climbing out of bed, she went over to look at them, hoping to find something good to read. Lifting each book, she read the titles: *The Love We Had, How to Make Love to A Man, The Path to Sensuous Sex, The Dummies' Guide to Earth Shattering Orgasms Every Night.*

With a deep, cooling intake of breath, DeAndra backed away from the dresser. No help there. She paced back and forth like a caged animal. Reaching her fingers up to her shoulders, she massaged the tight coil of tense muscles. Finally, she drew the sensible cotton gown on over the bikini in case she encountered Damon and left the room.

Most of the lights were off except for the occasional nightlight plugged in close to the baseboards to keep people from tripping in the dark. In the great room, she found Damon sprawled in a recliner next to one of the sofas. He had a glass of amber liquid in his hands and stared off into space.

She wanted to go to him, climb in his lap, and press herself against him, but she wasn't sure of her reception. She'd always thought of Damon as hers, but Imani had shown her that was not true. She wanted to comfort him. Instead she simply stood there.

Damon focused on her. "Hey," he said, his gaze taking in her gown and bare feet. "I suppose you couldn't sleep either?"

"No," she answered, wondering at the strange vibes he was giving off. She'd never seen this mood on Damon and she didn't know how to take it.

"Sit down, have a drink," he said, waving her towards the sofa. I don't bite, at least not yet."

DeAndra poured herself a glass of wine. Then she took a seat on the couch.

CHAPTER ELEVEN

Watching DeAndra from his spot in the enormous, leather recliner, Damon could see the sleek dark outlines of a thong and skimpy bra beneath the conservative cotton gown. He could almost imagine what they looked like. DeAndra used to wear the most skimpy and provocative undergarments, especially when she was trying to take his mind off his ex-fiancée, Imani.

Damon gave himself a mental shake. Since when had he been reduced to imagining what lay beneath a woman's clothes? He tried for honesty and integrity in everything he did, but he didn't know how to proceed with DeAndra. He'd missed her in his life and wanted her with him now, not just to keep her safe, but also because he enjoyed her. From the moment she'd walked into the house, the urge to take her to bed had never been far from his thoughts.

DeAndra took a seat on the couch, her delicate facial features scrubbed clean of makeup. "Damon, what's the matter?" she asked as she set her wineglass on the coffee table.

"Nothing," he answered from his spot in the recliner, "and everything." His mood was strange and would have been better kept to himself, but he couldn't bring himself to send DeAndra away. He enjoyed her company too much for that.

"What are you thinking?" she prompted, lifting the glass to her lips to take a sip.

He regarded her silently for several moments. "I've been thinking about what we did today and how brave you were, about my life, the way it was, and the way it is now. I've been enjoying my life by living through my work and it has to stop."

"What would you do differently?" she asked, leaning towards him, still sipping her wine.

"Live, get a personal life. As they say, 'get me some business.'"

"And would that have an impact on the things you do with me?" she asked carefully. She tried for nonchalance in her tone and facial expression, but Damon saw the vulnerability underneath.

"Do you want it to?" he asked, sensing that he was stepping onto uncharted ground.

DeAndra nodded. "I fight it," she admitted, biting her lip. "I've been fighting it for years, but we both know what I want."

Just hearing the implication of her words made his pulse jump. "What do you want?" he asked, studying her lazily as his fingers curved around his glass.

She swallowed, gathering her courage, and then her soft voice filled the room like a siren's song. "I want you, Damon."

"I want you too," he admitted. "You're a beautiful, vibrant, and intelligent woman and you've been driving me crazy. I haven't had a good night's sleep since you've been here."

"Me either. Oh, Damon!" In one fluid movement, she stood and drew the gown up over her head and off.

As she tossed it to the floor, the image of her standing before him in the thin string bikini burned itself into his brain. The tiny bra lifted her full breasts, but the chocolate-colored tips of her breasts were still visible through the thinly-woven fabric.

She gracefully twirled around on her ruby-painted toenails and he saw a ruby glinting on a gold loop from her navel above the soft swell of her abdomen. The bikini bottom barely covered the triangle between her shapely thighs, the back of it merely a loop around the flirtatious curve of her butt.

Damon sat up in the recliner, blood strumming through his veins, making his ears ring. He fumbled with the buttons on his shirt, virtually ripping it open. He had on too many clothes. His erection pushed against the front of his pants.

Before he could get out of his shirt, she was on his lap, straddling him in the recliner. The fragrant scent of DeAndra mixed with a flowery shower gel filled his nostrils, pumping him up, making him dizzy. "You smell so good," he whispered.

The answering seductive smile that lit her face made his blood sizzle. Tracing the fullness of her lips, he dipped his tongue into the sweetness of her mouth and stayed to savor long, drugging kisses. Her soft moans sent thrills of excitement coursing through him.

"Damon", she whispered, her body trembling.

He felt the moist heat of her mound tight against his erection as she leaned forward, unbuckling his belt. Damn, she was hot! His hands trembled. His pants tightened painfully.

Under her determined ministrations, the zipper gave suddenly, relieving him of the restraint. With soft, hot hands, she slipped her hand into his briefs to touch him.

"Aaaargh!" Flexing within those soft, teasing hands, he almost lost it. His breath came out in a heavy groan. "Wait, let me see you, let me touch you," he begged.

"I'm yours, Damon, all yours," she murmured, leaning forward to rest against his bare chest.

His hands touched her soft, silky skin, cupping the globes of her breasts and tracing their hardened tips beneath the thin mesh. Her soft moans excited him. He slid his hands down past her waist to gently knead the voluptuous curve of her buttocks and cup her mound. DeAndra was petite, but her curves were lush. His fingers slipped beneath the soaked edge of the thong to dip into her hot center.

She gasped, rotating her hips and pressing herself against him. "Do me, Damon, do me right now!" she begged.

Hearing the words, looking at her, and touching her so intimately made him want to explode. He laid her down in the recliner and stepped out of his pants. Throwing off his shirt, he leaned over her and pulled down the thin bra to burn a path of open-mouthed kisses from her lips and neck to the chocolate-colored tips of her breasts. He laved them, sucking them, while his fingers moved in and out of her center in a wild rhythm that had her panting and crying out his name. She stiffened suddenly, her body shaking, and her essence flowed over his fingers and down her thighs.

Driven by a desire entirely new to him, he traced a path to her navel with his tongue, circling the delicate fold, and continuing on to press warm kisses against the soft swell of her undulating abdomen. He kissed the insides of her thighs, tasting the essence that lingered there and then boldly removed her thong to kiss her intimately. DeAndra convulsed against him in a tangle of moist caramel thighs and scented skin.

Eyes alight with wonder, she lay in the recliner, thanking him, telling him how good it had been. Extending both hands, she dragged off his briefs and welcomed him back into the moist cradle of her thighs, then her tight channel. With a sudden loss of control, he thrust into her with a primitive rhythm. She wrapped her legs around his waist, holding on, passionately rocking with him until they both hit a sharp peak and shuddered their way back to earth.

Afterward, they lay together, kissing and touching each other over and over again in wonder. Damon felt dazed. DeAndra had tears in her eyes as she told him how happy she was.

When they grew cold in the recliner, Damon took her by the hand and led her to his bedroom. There, in the enormous bed, they made love again. Afterward, DeAndra curled up against him and fell asleep.

For a while Damon lay in the dark, his body sated. He still felt as if he were floating. Making love with DeAndra was more intense and pleasurable than anything he'd ever experienced. It had been like that, even when he'd been going through all the drama with Imani. To his shame, he had used DeAndra as an antidote to Imani.

Curving his body tighter around hers, he inhaled the fragrant scent of her hair and let his hands caress her silky skin. Now that she had matured and he'd gotten over his infatuation with Imani, he hoped they could ride out the intense attraction they shared.

In the park, she sat at a picnic table beneath a large maple tree. She wore a cap, dark glasses and held a newspaper, pretending to read. Her hands were sweaty. Because she was nervous, it was hard to sit still and pretend a relaxed casualness she didn't feel. She glanced at her watch, wondering if she would see him today. He hadn't been into the office in days. After what she'd done, she'd avoided his house, but now she needed to see him, and see if he still loved her.

As if on cue, she saw a tall, lean man running in the distance. He was about the right height and weight. As he drew closer, she recognized his favorite blue jogging pants and one of the matching jackets with white stripes. It was he.

Biting the insides of her cheeks, she kept herself from smiling. Anticipation prickled across her skin as she drank in the sight of him, ignoring the figure to his left, a little farther up the trail, and the shorter male figure that trailed several lengths behind him. She wasn't concerned with them because he was a man who always jogged alone, and he was competitive enough that by the time he reached her, the others would be far behind.

As she waited for him, she wondered if he was angry about the things she'd done? Yes, he had to be. She'd virtually destroyed his place. But what value did material things have when he had the benefit of a love like hers? If he loved her the way he should, he would be able to forgive anything. She was the one who should be angry. After all, he'd ignored her since he'd been back. Hell, with a love like theirs, why was she meeting him in the park anyway?

She felt the anger growing inside her like a dark cloud blocking out the sunlight. Her lips poked out with it, one hand closing in an impotent fist. It threatened to consume her as her fingers closed on the smooth object in her pocket. He didn't deserve her love. Maybe someone should teach him a lesson. Her eyes narrowed as he closed the distance between them and she came to a decision. She was just the woman to do it.

Her hand closed on the glass cylinder and she used the cover of her paper to carefully remove the stopper. When he was close enough to touch, he ran on, like a stranger, instead of greeting her. She stood, and dashed the contents of the cylinder in the direction of his chest and arms. She didn't want to mess up that handsome face.

Instinctively, he veered to the side, throwing up his arms to protect his vulnerable face and chest, but it was too late for that beautiful chest and those broad shoulders. His scream of pain tore the air, and she pictured skin shriveling up, being eaten away. He tried to grab her, but his agony was so great that she avoided him easily.

She felt strangely satisfied and vindicated, as he tore at his clothes and jumped around like a wild thing on fire. Suppressing a triumphant giggle, she shouted, "You don't deserve me!" She thought she saw his green eyes widen beneath the dark glasses.

The other runners were shouting and running towards them. With a burst of speed, she ran off into the woods and down a trail to her waiting car. One of the men followed, but she had a good head start. Safely inside, she drove out the other end of the park, passing the approaching police cars. She laughed, on a high from the adventure and all that she had accomplished.

Morning brought the first faint hints of light and the feel of DeAndra on top of him, rubbing her soft body along his like a sensuous cat.

117

"DeAndra," he murmured, sliding his hands down her waist to cup the curve of her bare behind. "Lady, I believe you are insatiable."

She nuzzled his face, her lips barely brushing his. "Is that a complaint?"

"Never, my lady. I live to serve," he quipped in a subservient voice.

"Well, you certainly have the proper equipment for it," she remarked, pressing herself against his erection and then moving to straddle him. "Such...nice...equipment," she sighed, slowly impaling herself upon him. Groaning, they began a slow, grinding rhythm.

A sharp ringing penetrated their sensual haze, a persistent alarm that was ultimately too much to ignore. Their movement slowed, then all but stopped as Damon reached for the phone, grumbling under his breath. "Hello?"

"Damon, you all right?" Clay's voice sounded tense.

"I'm good. Would have been even better if you could have held off calling me for another twenty minutes."

"So, it's like that, huh?" Clay's voice lightened a little, as if he were pleased to have interrupted Damon's pleasure. "What's her name?"

"We're not going there." Damon stroked the length of DeAndra's back, fighting the feeling of foreboding that was stealing over him. "What's up, Clay? Something happen? This is the first time you've called me since I've been here."

"I've got bad news." Clay's voice dipped low in pitch and volume.

Damon tensed. He saw that DeAndra was looking at him, with something akin to fear growing in her wide eyes. "Let me have it."

"Dennis and the crew went out on your run early this morning. Some woman was waiting for him in the park. Just as soon as he got close, she threw acid on him!"

"No!" Damon's fingers gripped the phone hard. "Is Dennis okay? He wasn't scarred for life?"

DeAndra gasped, moving closer in an effort to hear more of the conversation.

"Dennis is in the hospital with burns to his arms and chest," Clay said, "Luckily, she wasn't aiming for his face. He'll make a full recovery, but it'll take a while."

"I feel responsible for this," Damon said, his pulse speeding up as he imagined what it must have been like for the undercover officer, "If he hadn't been pretending to be me, he'd be okay."

Clay's voice took on a cutting note. "Damon, it's his job. We didn't plan for him to get hurt, but it happened. I personally chewed the hell out of his team for falling too far behind to apprehend the woman."

"You didn't get her?" Damon's voice took on an incredulous tone.

"One of the team chased after her while the other got the first aid kit from the car to tend to Dennis and then called an ambulance. This woman ran into the thick part of the woods and disappeared. She obviously had a car stashed away somewhere."

"Give me the info on Dennis," Damon said. "I want to send some flowers."

"Don't waste your money," Clay admonished. Dennis spends a lot of time down on that gun range on Dequindre. He calls it gun therapy. I happened to know he'd like more, but can't afford it."

"Okay, I'll get him some time." Damon stroked the area above his lips and down to his chin. "Does Dennis have a wife and kids?"

"No wife or kids. Damon, that's enough. The man was doing his job. I figure that by now, you're probably getting a little antsy. You've got to stay low, man. We're dealing with a crazy woman. There's no telling what she'll do next."

"What am I supposed to do?" Damon asked. "I can't stay in Chicago forever."

"Just be patient, man. We're going to catch this woman."

"How? Did your guys even get a good look at her?"

The long silence preceding Clay's next words spoke volumes. "She had on a hat, big jacket and glasses. We know that she could be a light-skinned African American or a tanned Caucasian, medium weight and height."

Damon paused, trying to remember everyone who'd ever threatened him. His chest felt so heavy that he could barely breathe. Being a judge automatically made some people his enemies, mainly lawbreakers. It was something he'd learned to deal with. "I can't think of anyone specific who might match that description."

"It's all right, Damon. We're going to catch her with another trap. If I have my way, it'll be within the next two weeks, okay?"

Damon ran a nervous finger over his mouth and chin. "I guess so. Seems like I don't really have much choice."

Clay's voice rose. "Oh yes, you do. You can choose life, man, by following my advice."

"I'm with you on this," Damon said, forcing the words. "I'll stick with the program."

When he ended the call and replaced the phone, DeAndra scooted higher to fold him into her arms, her face against his. There were elements of fear in her brown eyes. "Damon, I don't want anything to happen to you."

"We're quite a pair, aren't we?" he said with a touch of irony. "You've got someone shooting into your car, and I have a stalker. What are we going to do?"

"I wish we could escape to a secret paradise, just the two of us. Then we could be safe."

He traced the delicate arch of her brows with a fingertip. "But we wouldn't be living in the real world, would we?"

"No." Her answer was close to a whisper. She pressed a kiss on his mouth. "I'm going to take a shower and get dressed."

She moved away from him. He felt the bed dip and spring back as she got up and went into the bathroom.

Damon lay on his side, thinking about his job, his office, and his friends. Except for the fact that he and DeAndra were together, he missed his life. Yes, he'd been lonely, but he'd only recently come to realize that fact.

Listening to the sound of DeAndra singing in the shower, he smiled and made a decision to enjoy the next two weeks to the fullest. After that, he was going to have to do something to get his life back. Hiding out in Chicago forever was not an option. He had a sworn duty to dispense justice in a timely manner.

DeAndra waltzed out of the bathroom, wrapped in his bathrobe, looking fresh. She hurried towards the bedroom door. "It's already after eight o'clock. I've got to hurry if I'm to make court by nine-thirty."

Startled out of his reflections, he did a double take. "You're going to court today?"

He could see her preparing herself for an argument. She stiffened, her eyes steeling with determination. "Yes. I told you that I had a couple of cases scheduled for today. I'm not going to let my clients down."

Propping himself up on an elbow, he said, "Even if it could mean your life? DeAndra, someone out there was trying to kill you."

She shook her head, denying his words. "We don't know for sure," she stammered, "Bruce said that he thought it might have been more of a warning, especially since they shot through the passenger side of the windshield."

He sat up in bed, letting the covers pool around his waist. "What if whoever shot at you was simply a bad shot?"

Her brows went up and she took her bottom lip between her teeth. "I don't have time to stand here and argue with you, Damon. I'm going and I don't need your permission."

In a huff, she turned and yanked open the door.

"You might need my car to get you there," he couldn't help reminding her. He had no intention of driving her to court, especially since someone could be waiting there to finish her off.

"Huh!" She stepped out into the hall, her shoulders straight and stiff. "Thanks but no thanks. This is Chicago, Damon. I can get there on the train."

He watched her march off to her room. Lifting the telephone receiver from the nightstand, he made two quick calls. Then he pulled the covers back and leapt out of bed. He hadn't been offering to drive and DeAndra knew it, but if she were going to deliberately put herself in danger, he would be there to catch her when she fell on that stubborn head.

Taking a quick but thorough shower, he dried off and zipped through his morning routine. Hustling out of the bathroom in a towel, he stood in closet, trying to find the right suit among the three he'd worn in Washington. Settling for a golden brown that would be less conspicuous, he found accessories and dressed in a hurry.

He found DeAndra sitting at the table in the kitchen, looking summery in her lemon yellow suit and matching Ferragamo sling backs. Drinking coffee and eating a raisin bagel with cream cheese, she glanced up as he entered, surprised that he'd also showered and dressed. "You going somewhere?"

"Yes. With you." Damon poured himself coffee and took one of the bagels from the bag on the table.

"Why? You don't want me to go."

He took the seat across from her. "No, I don't, but I refuse to let you go alone."

She set her empty cup on the table. "Then I hope you're ready to leave real soon. I can't afford to be late. I'm leaving in five minutes."

Damon sipped his coffee, letting the bitter brew shock his system into edgy alertness. "You might be leaving before that," he murmured reaching for a napkin.

"Excuse me?" She leaned toward him, a puzzled look on her face.

The blast of a car horn sounded twice, just outside the house Damon stood and went over to the window and drew the curtain aside to look out. "That's for us. Come on, Dee, we don't want to be late."

Looking mildly annoyed, she stood, gathering her briefcase and purse. "I didn't need a ride, Damon. A cab down to court is going to be expensive."

"I'll pay for it." Going back to the table, he wrapped his bagel in the napkin and stuffed it in a pocket. "I figured that it would be quicker and safer than walking to the stop and waiting for the train and we won't have to worry about parking."

"Yeah." She put on a dark pair of sunglasses, hiding her eyes from view. Her heels clicked against the floor and her hips swayed sensuously as she made her way to the door. Following, Damon forced his thoughts to the alarm system needing to be set, the door, and the keys in his hand.

The ride was longer than he'd imagined, but he contented himself with the sight of parts of the city he'd never seen. DeAndra sat beside him and didn't utter a word. He hoped he was doing the right thing and prayed that today would be boring, with him waiting patiently while DeAndra tried her cases. He'd left the gun at home, but he'd taken out a little extra insurance on their safety.

CHAPTER TWELVE

As the taxi arrived at the Richard J. Daley Center, Damon pulled out his cell and punched in a series of numbers.

"You're paging someone at a time like this?" DeAndra asked incredulously.

He checked his watch. "We've got time. It's only five after nine." Digging his wallet out of an inside jacket pocket, he took his time paying the bill and tipping the driver.

"Can we get out now?" DeAndra asked, gathering her briefcase and purse.

From the outside, someone opened the door to the taxi. They turned to see who it was.

"Bruce!" DeAndra cried out in surprise. "I wasn't expecting to see you."

Damon exhaled in relief. He hadn't planned to exit the taxi without Bruce's help. He'd sensed Bruce's commitment to his job and the fact that he was a true friend to DeAndra.

Dressed in his police uniform, Bruce stepped aside so that Damon could exit the cab. "Hey there, Damon, DeAndra. Damon told me you were coming down here, so I decided to come out and help him make sure you got in safely."

Swallowing, she made a show of looking down at her briefcase and purse. Her eyes softened with moisture and she blinked quickly. Scooting carefully across the seat, she gave each man one of her bags and one of her hands to help her out of the cab. "Thank you, Bruce, Damon," she said, her voice wobbling a little while she exited gracefully. "I'm really blessed to have you two friends."

Damon and Bruce more or less shielded her with their bodies as they walked into the building. It was like something out of a movie. Damon's heart raced and a light sweat broke out on his forehead. He didn't know what he would do if DeAndra got hurt. People went in and out of the building in droves, talking, laughing, arguing, and complaining.

Damon zeroed in on a group protesting the trial of a neighborhood kid. They waved signs and were loud and aggressive in their movements and speech. One burly man pushed close enough to nearly separate Damon from DeAndra and Bruce, but Damon held his ground.

Switching his attention, Damon focused on people whose glances strayed a little too long, people with bulges in their pockets, and people who hit the suspicious-looking mark on his personal meter. He saw that Bruce's practiced professional eye kept moving through the crowd too. They didn't breathe a sigh of relief until they had gone through the metal detectors and made it to their floor at Cook County Circuit Court.

"I've got to go," Bruce told them. "I'm scheduled to testify in about half an hour."

Thanking him, they headed down to the courtroom where DeAndra was scheduled. Two clients and a tall blonde in a black suit, an associate from the law firm, were waiting for DeAndra. She quickly introduced Damon to the agency lawyer, Nadia, and her clients, Mr. Barrels and Mrs. Payne. When they began to compare notes and talk strategy, Damon took a seat in the audience.

DeAndra's first case was second on the docket. Seeing her in action only confirmed what he'd known for a long time; she was a damned good lawyer. It took all of an hour. With strategic questioning and presentation of the evidence, she persuaded a judge that a mortgage company had foreclosed on her client illegally. The ecstatic woman was so happy that she cried, hugging DeAndra and Nadia effusively. Damon followed them out of the courtroom and to the clerk's office where they filled out the appropriate paperwork.

In an effort to tone down the edginess that was making him restless, Damon switched to decaffeinated coffee. By the time they made it back to the courtroom, the next case was over and the judge adjourned for lunch.

"How about some lunch?" he asked as the courtroom rapidly emptied.

DeAndra shifted her purse up onto her arm. "Sure, I know a place, Baxter's. You can get a sandwich and I can get a salad."

"Great, I could use some food about now." Damon took charge of her briefcase and followed her out of court.

Baxter's was a cozy deli-style restaurant in the Daly Center. The lunch crowd practically jammed the place. Luckily, they spotted Bruce and his partner at a table in the back, and squeezed in to join them for lunch.

Bruce introduced them to his partner, Adam, and then everyone ordered from the menu. They sat drinking soda and talking until Bruce turned their attention to the big screen television in a corner of the bar. A picture of Mouse covered the screen.

"Have you seen this child?" the news anchor asked, "This is ten-year-old Michelle Brown. She's been missing for about a week. Police say that she disappeared a day after receiving a brutal beating from her uncle. If you have seen her or have any information that might help the police locate her, please call 555-1234."

When the news anchor moved on to another story, they all looked at each other.

Damon still saw the image of a little girl with two braids, a wide toothy smile, and eyes which held a poignant hope. With what he knew of the things that had happened to her, all he could do was pray she had survived.

"That's the first time I've seen that on the news," DeAndra remarked, excitement growing in her brown eyes. "Maybe you guys will get some new leads."

Damon kept his thoughts to himself, but Bruce nodded, his expression grave. "Maybe. That reminds me that I meant to call back to the lab and see if they got a match on those fingerprints." Rising, he went off to make a call.

The food arrived. Damon bit into his corned beef and pastrami sandwich and DeAndra dug into her fried chicken salad, while Adam wolfed down a burger.

Bruce returned minutes later, a satisfied expression on his face. "Good news," he said, taking his seat and tasting his clam chowder. "The prints on the shells in your car match those on the gun found at the Browns' house. They also match those on file for Eric Brown, Michelle's uncle."

Damon had halfway expected as much, but confirmation brought relief. His glance met Bruce's and then centered on DeAndra, who'd dropped her fork.

She gasped audibly. "I knew the man disliked me on sight, but to try to kill me?"

"Unless there's something you forgot to tell me, it all goes back to intimidation," Bruce said. "With you raising the alarm by asking all those questions, he was bound to go to jail for child abuse once we found his niece. With the prints we have, he'll get picked up today."

She wet her lips. "That means I can go home now, right?"

Damon tensed at the question. Was DeAndra anxious to get away from him? She'd been acting as if she was enjoying herself.

"No," Bruce said, answering her question. "Not until we've picked him up. I'll call you when it's done, but until then, stay with Damon."

As she nodded in agreement, Damon relaxed for the moment. He couldn't imagine being in the condo without DeAndra. She'd brought a lot of adventure, excitement, companionship, and romance with her, things that had been missing in his life. It went without saying that he would miss her.

Having come back into his life when she was threatened, Damon wondered if DeAndra would stay, now that she was safe. He knew that he needed her, whether what they'd been doing was really best for the both of them or not. Just then their gazes met and he would have sworn that she was wrestling with the same issue.

After lunch, Damon followed DeAndra back to the courtroom, but realized that he'd had enough of second guessing the judge from the sidelines. DeAndra's next case was going to be the second of the afternoon. When they made preparations to begin, he went off, promising to return before court adjourned.

Walking the Daly Center, he was relieved to be near closure on the threat to DeAndra's life. His mind refused to contemplate the way the rest of the day would go. Finding a florist, he ordered flowers for Dennis Robertson, and had them sent to Receiving Hospital in Detroit. Then he called the gunnery that Robertson used in Michigan and paid for range time for Dennis. Afterward, he simply walked the complex, like a rat in a maze.

When Damon made it back to court, Nadia, DeAndra, and Barells were all hugging and congratulating each other on their success. The judge had adjourned court for the day.

Retrieving her briefcase and purse, DeAndra joined him at the back of the room.

"Congratulations, counselor," he said, basking in the warmth of her wide smile as he shook her hand. "You did some good work today."

She let him take her briefcase. "Thanks. I'm so happy, I could break out in a dance right here. I just knew they had us on this one, but I dug my heels in anyway, and voilà!"

"Have they picked up Eric Brown yet?" he asked.

Pulling a cell phone from her purse, she checked for messages. "I didn't get a call from Bruce."

"Then let's go back to the house," he said, taking her arm. He suppressed the little lift he got from knowing that DeAndra would be staying with him at least one more night.

Despite the news of Eric Brown's imminent arrest, Damon's felt nervous as he led DeAndra from the building and hustled her into a cab. At the house, he paid the driver, then made a visual sweep of their surroundings before helping her from the cab.

Inside, he turned to lock the door as she dropped her briefcase in a corner. When he turned around, she was in his arms in one forward motion, with her face against his chest. He could feel her shaking slightly. "Are you okay?" he asked.

Her head bobbed up and down. "I just needed a hug real bad. It's been a hell of a day."

"You're right about that," he said, thinking about the suspenseful arrival at the courthouse and getting into the building. He knew that she'd fought hard to win her cases too. Inhaling the spicy scent of her cologne, he smoothed his hands down her back and gently massaged her shoulders. Then he held her close. "You had a great day in court, despite being worried about your friend."

Her head moved up and down against his chest. "Going to court and coming back out was pretty scary too," she admitted. "You think I'm so brave, Damon, and you're wrong. Believe me, I was shaking in my boots the whole time."

"Being brave isn't about how you feel when you're doing what has to be done; it's about doing what's required in spite of your feelings," he said.

"When that guy almost separated us, I could have screamed," she confessed.

"I nearly had a heart attack myself," he admitted, "I couldn't live with myself if something happened to you and I let it happen."

They hugged each other closer. After a moment, she lifted her head to press a kiss to his cheek. When he turned his cheek, their lips came together in a kiss that started with an affectionate touch of the lips and intensified into something that sent shivers of desire coursing through them.

When they broke apart, they were both breathing hard. They stared at each other. He noted the rise and fall of her chest and the sensual intensity in her eyes. His heart raced as he fought the urge to drag her into his bedroom to have his way with her. He hadn't felt this horny in years. The moment stretched on till Damon realized that she was holding back.

"Maybe we should fix something to eat," Damon suggested finally, clamping down on his hormones. He wasn't going to push her into anything.

"Yeah, I'm starving. Just let me change my clothes," she said, wetting her lips and moving away from him. "I'll do the chicken if you do the vegetables."

"You've got a deal." He headed for his room.

DeAndra changed into jeans and a V-neck top and stepped into her tennis shoes. First to make it to the kitchen, she washed her hands, located the raw chicken in the refrigerator and washed it. Then she sprinkled it with seasoned salt and pepper, shook it up in a bag full of flour, and placed the pieces a frying pan filled with hot oil. She'd placed a cover on the pan and washed her hands again when Damon appeared in an old pair of Dockers and a blue muscle shirt.

"Boy, you're fast. I can smell that chicken already," he quipped, washing his hands at the sink.

Her eyes strayed time and again to his handsome face, the smooth brown chest and wide shoulders revealed by the muscle shirt. He'd always fascinated her. Now that she'd decided to let herself enjoy this time, it felt good just being around him, being able touch him and kiss him. She was living a dream she'd had for years. The only snake in this garden was the fact that she couldn't let herself get addicted to Damon.

He'd all but admitted that although he cared for her, the sexual chemistry between them was what had brought him to her arms.

Tearing her gaze away, she switched on the kitchen fan. "It just started cooking, so it'll be awhile." She found a pair of tongs in one of the drawers, then dragged a stool from a corner and sat down on it.

Damon opened each cabinet, scanned the contents, and closed them again. He did the same with the refrigerator. Then he started over again.

"Green beans?" she suggested. "Broccoli? How about a salad?"

"I just want something different." Damon went back to the refrigerator and drew a package of fresh Brussels sprouts from the vegetable bin. Washing each one carefully, he put them on the stove to steam.

DeAndra thought about tomorrow and what she would do. The police were sure to have arrested Eric Brown by tomorrow. She would be able to go to work and back to her condo, and there would be no reason to stay here with Damon. *Unless he asks me to stay.* She ignored the thought. That wasn't going to happen.

Damon went back to the refrigerator. Producing a few ears of fresh corn, he set them on the counter. She shucked two for him, throwing the waste in the basket and carefully peeling off the corn silk. Placing them back on the counter, she saw that Damon was just finishing his two. Her mouth spread into a smile.

"Think we should open a restaurant?" he teased, washing the corn and placing the ears into salted boiling water.

"I don't know," she said, playing along. "I've got to taste test the food first." Rising, she checked on the chicken and turned the pieces on the other side. Then she found a Riesling in the refrigerator and two wine glasses in one of the cabinets. "Want some wine?"

"Sure, I'll have some." Grabbing plates and a handful of silverware, he began to set the table.

The cork slid smoothly out of the bottle. Proud of herself, she poured two glasses and placed them on the table. Then she put the deep brown, crispy chicken on paper towels to drain.

"My mouth is watering," he said as he dipped up the corn and Brussels sprouts.

DeAndra laughed. On a whim, she switched on the fancy radio/CD player that was built in under the cabinet. The room was suddenly filled with the romantic sounds of Luther Vandross' "Here and Now." She turned to look at Damon, who was busy putting the food on the table.

He caught her glance, shrugged, and smiled. "What can I say? I'm a romantic guy."

"Don't say anything." She took her seat at the table. "I *like* romantic guys." *And I love you, even if I have promised myself I'd never say that to you again.*

Her heart beat faster when he turned down the lights and lit a couple of candles, but she held in the sigh when he sat down and took her hand.

"Shall we say a prayer of thanks?" he asked.

Nodding, she closed her eyes and let the mellow sound of his voice wash over her as he thanked the Lord for their safety, her success in court, and the meal they'd prepared. Then she opened her eyes and they began to eat.

The meal was simple but good. Enjoying their food and each other, they relaxed. They laughed and talked about things they'd done in the past and things they wanted to do. Damon revealed that he'd always wanted to take a trip to Egypt and DeAndra revealed a longing to go to Hawaii.

"Maybe we'll both get our wishes," Damon chuckled, sipping his wine.

The telephone rang. They sat there a moment, almost willing it to stop. When it didn't, Damon got up and answered.

From the part of the conversation DeAndra heard, she knew that Bruce Moran was on the other end of the line and that there was good news. She got up from the table and hurried over. "Have they found Mouse? Is she okay?"

Damon's head dipped. "No, it's not about Mouse." He gave her the phone.

She spoke into the receiver. "Hello?"

Bruce's voice sounded in her ear. "Good news, Dee. We've got Eric Brown in custody. You can go on home now and into work tomorrow."

Her shoulders slumped with overwhelming relief and a tear rolled down her cheek. "That's great, Bruce! Now I can get back to my life. You know it was pretty scary out there today."

Bruce Moran's voice was tinged with concern. "Yes, I know, Dee. That's why I called you right away. You gonna be all right?"

DeAndra wiped away another tear. "I'm fine. Just a little emotional. I feel like I've been on a roller coaster."

Damon put a comforting arm around her shoulders.

"Okay. Take care of yourself, then, and give me a call sometime tomorrow," Bruce ordered.

"All right, Bruce. Thanks again." She hung up the phone.

Damon stood close behind her. He dropped his arm. "Do you want me to take you home?"

His voice held a low, caressing quality. She turned to face him. Looking into those beautiful green eyes, she realized that he wanted her to stay. "Not yet," she managed.

He moved closer to cup her face in his hands. His fingers trailed down to stroke her neck, sending shivers through her. "Stay. Stay with me tonight," he whispered.

She lifted her face and his lips met hers with a hot, scorching demand. Trembling under the passionate onslaught, she opened her mouth and returned kiss for kiss, reveling in the feel of his hands on her breasts and buttocks. He trailed hot, open-mouthed kisses down her neck and deep into her cleavage to suckle her aching nipples. Her stomached dropped and she began to melt inside. Moaning, she curled into him.

"Is that a yes?" he whispered against her skin.

Their gazes met. The hungry, sensual look in his eyes nearly stole her breath. "Yes," she breathed.

"Good, 'cause I couldn't have held out much longer!" He lifted her into his arms and carried her into his bedroom.

She laid her head against his warm chest, daydreaming of what was to come. He didn't disappoint her. He removed each piece of her clothing and covered every inch of her bare skin with hot, reckless kisses. When he pulled on protection, she spread her legs and welcomed him. Their gazes locked as he pushed his hardened thickness so deep inside her that they both shot halfway to heaven.

She closed her eyes. A firestorm of heady sensations took her as he thrust in and out of her, establishing a glorious rhythm that carried them higher and higher until they convulsed together, shivering with ecstasy.

In the aftermath, Damon pulled her close, nestling his body against hers, spoon fashion. His lips brushed her cheek.

"*That* was wonderful," she sighed. She felt more than heard his answering chuckle against her hair. Turning, she kissed him, lingering and savoring the taste of his mouth. "Do you believe in equal time?"

Before he could answer, she trailed kisses across the curve of his jaw and down his neck. "My turn," she purred against his skin. She felt his quick intake of breath as she lingered on his chest and moved lower. When the game came to its inevitable conclusion, they lay together and fell asleep.

CHAPTER THIRTEEN

DeAndra awakened from a deep sleep, and looked at the clock. It was already seven-thirty. She hopped out of bed and hunted for her clothes in the semi-darkness. Her top and slacks were on the floor near the bed, but her underwear was nowhere to be found. Giving up, she turned on the light in the bathroom and left the door ajar to avoid turning on a lamp and disturbing Damon. Locating her underwear on the other side of the bed, she gathered her things, turned off the bathroom light, and left to shower in her own room.

As the melody from Luther Vandross' "Here and Now" played over and over in her head, she began to sing. The hot spray soothed the tender areas of her body.

Stepping out of the shower, feeling energized and ready to take on the world, she went through her routine and donned the navy suit she'd worn when she encountered Damon at Mort's Deli. Buttoning the front, she decided it was a good thing they'd had it cleaned since it was the only thing she had with her that was suitable for work.

Picking her hair out with her fingers, she applied liquid foundation to her face and added a little lipstick, eyeliner, and mascara. Back in the bedroom, she carefully folded everything and placed the items back in the shopping bags.

One glance at the bedside clock, and she was hurrying again. Leaving her clothes on the bed, she scurried to the kitchen for a cup of coffee.

The light was on in the kitchen, and the scent of fresh coffee filled the air. The early morning news provided a backdrop of informative noise. Blinking, she saw Damon in a gold and black version of the sophisticated robes men wore in the movies, only his ended at the knees. The sight of his strong, athletic legs and the tantalizing trail of hair on his chest drew her attention again and again.

He poured a cup of coffee, added cream and sugar, and handed it to her. As she settled at the table with it, he set a small bowl of fruit salad and a fork in front of her. She smiled, touched that he'd remembered. "Thanks."

He nodded. "I couldn't send you off without something to eat."

Lifting the fork, she began to eat her salad, relishing the sweet taste of ripe strawberries, sliced banana, fresh pineapple chunks and Granny Smith apple slices. "Are you going to have some?" she asked, feeling a little guilty for putting him to so much trouble.

"Later. Much later. I'm planning to go back to bed, once you've gone to work." He came closer, his expression changing as a new thought occurred. "Unless you'd like me to drive you to work?"

The thought stirred up pleasant pictures, but she had imposed on Damon enough. "No, but thanks. That's not necessary. I'm taking the train. It'll have me there in no time."

"Can I get you anything else?" He stifled a yawn, muscles tensing and bringing back memories of their late, passion-filled night.

DeAndra couldn't resist letting her gaze linger on a few strategic spots on his body.

Damon burst into seductive laughter. "You're good for my ego, I'll tell you that. If you didn't have to go to work, I could think of a few new things to try…"

His hand curved against her cheek. She rubbed her cheek against it and stood. "I guess I'll just have to come back."

"I guess you will," he murmured, pulling her into his arms.

She rested her cheek against his chest, listening to his heartbeat.

Abruptly, the running background dialog from the television penetrated her thoughts with the words 'missing child.' Turning to check the screen, she saw a news reporter standing outside the abandoned home where she and Damon had found Mouse's pen.

The reporter began her commentary. "A woman who lives several blocks away from the little girl's family has come forward and told police that when she saw some of the neighborhood children going in and out of an abandoned home, she investigated. There she found a child she can now identify as Michelle Brown lying on a pallet in an upstairs bedroom. She told police that the child had been so severely beaten that she had a black eye, several bruises, and a broken arm. Being a nurse, the woman took the child into her home and did what she could to treat her injuries. Because the child became upset when the woman tried to get information to notify her family or child protection officials, she decided to wait until the child became comfortable with her."

"Michelle stayed at the woman's house for about a day and a half. Then she ran away when the Good Samaritan went to the basement to do laundry. At that point, which was three days ago, the Good Samaritan reported the incident to the police. If you have information that could help police locate this child, please call 555-1234. Chyna Walters reporting for Action News."

"I don't know if this is good news or bad," DeAndra muttered, turning back to Damon.

"At least you know that she was all right a few days ago," he reminded her.

"Yes, but where is she now? If I were Mouse, I'd come to me or her grandma's house."

"Does she know where you live?"

"Not really. I just moved. I'm going to call around on my lunch hour and see if I can't get hold of her grandmother. From little things Mouse has said, I know she's in the phone book. It wouldn't hurt to call."

Pivoting to grab several items off the counter, he started putting the leftover fruit back into the refrigerator. "It wouldn't hurt, but you'd think the police and Sonia would have covered that one by now."

"Yeah, but maybe she wasn't there at the time, and maybe Grandma is upset about what happened to Mouse. If it were me, I'd give Mouse a chance to recover."

"That could be." Finishing his task, he took a seat across from her at the table. She glanced at her watch. "I've got to go. Damon, I'll be back to get my things tonight."

"I could pick you up," he suggested casually. "Then we could get your car."

"Would you? That would be great. Damon, thank you for being the friend I needed by helping me and letting me stay. I really appreciate it." She pressed a kiss to his cheek. "Now I've really got to run."

With her purse on her shoulder and her briefcase in her hand, she turned and hurried off to work. As she'd discovered yesterday, the train stop from Damon's temporary place was the same one she used. Her new condo wasn't as ritzy as this one, but it was quite nice.

Somehow she hit the train right on time and managed to get to work and into her office within a minute of the scheduled time. Her desk was as she'd left it, but the desk of her officemate, Joyce, looked barren and empty. Joyce had been identified as a high potential junior partner and that group had been moved to a newly renovated part of the company offices.

Walking over to take a look at the stack of boxes stacked next to it. She read the name *Kerri Davis* on each box. She knew Kerri as one of the law clerks who'd spent two summers with the firm. DeAndra had been with the firm just about as long as a full-time associate had. At the very least, she should have advanced to one of the larger offices or received company perks in acknowledgement of her dedicated time and effort.

Feeling as though she'd been working hard and not being appreciated, she gritted her teeth and dug into the stack of files on her desk. Yes, the associates identified for the junior partner program had been with the company for a longer period of time, but DeAndra had a much better record of successes than several of them did. Shouldn't that count for something?

Instead of going out for lunch, DeAndra stayed in the office and asked a friend to pick up a salad for her while she used one of the people search sites on the internet to get a list of names and numbers. Then she made calls to Cleary, Alabama.

It took a while, but she finally dialed the number of the woman who was Mouse's grandmother. Her pleasant voice held distinct notes of suspicion. Awkward silences punctuated their conversation but DeAndra held on, making sure that Mrs. Brown knew exactly who she was. She talked about Mouse, what she did at the Legal Aid Center, and her talent for art. When she started to describe some of the pictures Mouse had done, Mrs. Brown's response warmed.

"I remember hearing about you, Ms. Blake. Michelle admires you, so she talks about you a lot. You have to understand I had to make sure it was you on the other end of the phone. I've gotten a lot of calls about my granddaughter in the last few days and some of them have been pretty weird."

DeAndra doodled on her notepad. "Mrs. Brown, have you seen your granddaughter?"

Mrs. Brown drew a long breath. "No, and I'm worried to death about that child. She's smart, but there's a lot of people out there just waiting to prey on children."

"I've been worrying about her too," DeAndra admitted, "No one seems to know where she's gone. Would you please let me know if you hear from her?"

Tears clogged the older woman's voice. "I'll do better than that. I'll let Michelle call you."

DeAndra swallowed. "Thank you, Mrs. Brown. You and your family are in my prayers."

Hanging up, DeAndra sipped a soft drink and ate her sandwich. *If*

Mouse was not at home or in the neighborhood, or at her grandmother's, where in the heck was she?

Surreptitiously, the woman watched the little girl at the sink washing her face and hands as best she could with one hand. The other was in an arm cast suspended in a graying sling. She'd seen the girl go into one of the stalls with a little packet of baby wipes only moments before. She admired those attempts at cleanliness. Lord knows it was hard enough to stay fresh and clean when you rode the bus for long hours.

Certain she'd seen the face somewhere, she studied it in the mirror, noting the fading bruise under one eye and the one on the left cheek. Someone had been abusing the girl. Where was the child's mother? Traveling in this day and age was bad enough without children being left on their own. "Are you traveling alone, honey?" she asked, breaking her usual habit of minding her own business.

The child's eyes widened, banked fear leaking into them. "M-My mother's picking me up at the next s-stop," she stammered.

Horrified that she had caused such distress, the woman turned to face the child, trying her best to appear non-threatening. "Honey, I'm not going to hurt you. I want to help. What's the matter? Has someone been bothering you?"

The child shook her head much too quickly and backed away. Her bottom lip quivered. She turned, ready to run.

Feeling guilty for frightening the child, the woman gave in to the urge to help. She dug into her pocket and pulled out a few bucks. "Here, honey. You hungry? Get yourself something to eat." She placed the money on the sink and moved away.

"T-thank you." The little girl grabbed the money off the sink with her free hand and scurried out of the bathroom.

Much, much later, the woman was at home watching the new

when one of the reporters did a repeat segment on a missing child. The woman stared at the face, excitement growing as she realized the face belonged to the little girl she'd seen in the bathroom at the bus station. Reaching for the phone, she dialed the number on the screen.

Working hard checking case references, DeAndra was startled by the buzzer on the phone. Shaking it off, she lifted the receiver.

"Judge Kessler is here to pick you up." The receptionist's voice rang with excitement.

DeAndra replaced the receiver, a smile on her lips. She could just see Damon out in the reception area, setting all the secretaries' hearts a-fluttering. Gathering all her papers and putting them back into the files, she stood and stretched. She retrieved her purse from a locked drawer, closed her briefcase and walked out of the office.

In the front lobby Damon, looking handsome and distinguished, was holding court all right; only the audience consisted of more than just the secretaries. Senior partners Len Sawyer and Tina Hatfield were standing at the reception desk talking to him. To see two of the partners, her bosses, busy kissing up to Damon did her heart good. She wondered if they were trying to get Damon to consider the firm when his term was up. Perhaps they even thought Damon was in town on a recruiting mission.

Tina glanced her way. "And here's DeAndra," she said brightly. "I know she used to clerk for you, Judge Kessler. Are you out scouting for new talent?"

Damon smiled gamely. "We're always looking for the *best* talent, counselor. DeAndra was among our best and brightest."

"Your loss was definitely our gain," Sawyer added. "She's headed for the fast track here."

That was news to DeAndra. Digesting that tidbit of information, she joined the group, greeting everyone.

"We were telling Judge Kessler how much we appreciate having you here," Tina said. "Your record of success on the important cases is among the best."

DeAndra smiled. "Thank you. I'm flattered to see that you've noticed my work. Would you say it compares favorably with that of the candidates for junior partnerships?"

Len Sawyer gave her one of those patronizing smiles. "If you'll schedule a meeting with my secretary, we can discuss this in detail tomorrow."

Clamping down hard on her instinctive negative reaction, she nodded. "Thank you. I'll do that."

Uttering cordial goodbyes, Damon and DeAndra left. By unspoken agreement, they were silent on the trip down the elevator and out the fancy front doors.

"Feeling unappreciated?" Damon asked as they stepped into the parking structure.

"Something like that." She let him take her arm as she carefully stepped over a rough section of the cement. "You're good at reading the vibes."

"I'm good at reading you." He released her arm as they made it to his car and he opened the trunk.

"I may end up with something extra, perks or cash for instance, just because you came to pick me up and they suspect you may be scouting," she said inanely, watching him store her briefcase slam the trunk. "That's the way they think around there."

Damon opened her door. "DeAndra, you deserve every penny they pay you and probably more. You're a brilliant attorney. If I never taught you anything else, I taught you to know your worth to your employers."

"I know my worth to the firm," she insisted. Settling onto the seat she buckled the seatbelt as he shut the door.

Damon climbed into the driver's seat and started the car. "If you know your worth, that means you've looked around."

She took her bottom lip between her teeth and then released it. "A little. Damon, I like the cases I get to work on, the leeway I have to get the job done, and the type of help available if I need it. I love working for this firm."

"Enough to become a partner and stay in Chicago forever?" Putting the car in gear he backed out of the parking space and drove towards the exit signs.

Turning the idea over in her thoughts, she shrugged. "I like the city."

"Then you'll have to find someone in Chicago to marry." His tone was flat and ominous sounding.

She turned to him, reading things into what he'd said but afraid to jump to conclusions. Was he thinking of marrying her sometime in the future? The thought made her feel all shaky inside because she could-n't think of anything she wanted more. He had never discussed mar-riage in relation to her because Imani had always loomed high on his radar.

Taking a deep breath, she let it out slowly. Then she spoke in as casual a tone as she could manage. "Damon, I know that long distance marriages are hard to maintain. The only reason we're together now is because we've both been threatened, but I've been so happy... Are you...thinking that you might want to get married sometime in the future?"

Damon's breath came out in a huff. "I don't want to get married. That's something that is *not* on my list. Going down that path only led to a lot of heartache and unhappiness. Now that I've finally gotten my life back, I'm not going there."

He gave her a quick glance, apparently reading something in the bland expression she projected with all of her might. "I hope I haven't said anything to hurt you," he said, already apologizing.

"You haven't," she managed, lying. Unshed tears and shattered dreams burned her eyes and clogged her throat, but she was not going to let him see it.

He turned onto Lakeshore Drive, glancing at her every few minutes or so to see her reaction to his words, make sure she wasn't upset. She made herself listen and hold it all in.

"I'm...glad we've been given this chance to explore the explosive chemistry between us," he continued. "It's an extra bonus because you have always been very dear to me. Years ago, you weren't as mature and I didn't understand what was going on."

"And that was?" She found her voice and it was cool and unemotional.

"We'd been suppressing the physical attraction we felt for each other. It had to be that way, of course, because you were seriously underage for several years after we met."

"That's true." Her father had abandoned her family so there'd been no male figure in her life. She'd bonded easily with Damon. He'd been her hero, the ideal man. She'd ignored her mother, but let Damon push, cajole, and inspire her into setting goals and changing her life. Was it any wonder that he was the love of her life?

DeAndra turned to look out the window. Late afternoon sun on the azure waters of Lake Michigan made it sparkle like precious jewels. She watched the tall, white masts of sailboats and several powerboats as they maneuvered the waters and thought about her life, her hopes, and dreams. One thing was inevitable; she needed to let go of the dream of marrying Damon and having his children.

"You're pretty quiet," he remarked as he stopped at a light.

"I'm just enjoying the scenery," she said. "I've had a long day."

"Did you manage to contact your friend's grandmother?"

Glad to have something else to focus on, she glanced at Damon. His expression was filled with concern as he accelerated.

DeAndra answered his question. "Yeah, but she hadn't seen Mouse

She said she'd let Mouse call me if she comes to Alabama."

Damon smiled. "I knew you would make contact with her because people are a priority with you. You have a big heart, DeAndra."

Turning back to the window, she lost herself in the passing scenery.

In the yard at the auto repair shop, Joss, her favorite mechanic, drooled over Damon's yellow Mercedes convertible and then teased her about Damon as he showed her the brand new windshield he'd installed. Examining it in detail, she decided that he'd done a fantastic job.

"Your car's been ready for at least a day and a half," Joss said.

Signing the insurance papers, DeAndra explained, "I couldn't come and get it right away."

"No problem," he teased, glancing meaningfully at Damon. "I can see you were busy."

"Cut the crap." DeAndra ripped off her copy of the insurance form and gave the clipboard back to him.

"Thank you. Anything else I can do for you folks?"

DeAndra stuck the insurance form into her purse. "No, we're good."

He raised an eyebrow. "I'll bet you are."

When DeAndra rolled her eyes, he smiled. "You folks have a nice day." Then he strolled back into the shop.

"Would you like to go to dinner?" Damon asked as the shop door closed.

She stood by her car, as she answered. "No, but thanks. I'm tired. I'm going to grab a salad and make an early night of it."

"Tired of me already?" he said, stepping closer, looking vulnerable.

She slanted him a glance. *You're unfair! I'm the one who's hurting from all the things you said.*

"I could never get tired of you, Damon," she quipped in a sassy tone. Two steps forward and she was in his arms with her head on his chest, hugging him tight. It felt so good that she could have stayed there forever with his arms around her. Unfortunately, the reality was that for Damon, it would never mean as much as it meant to her.

Tilting her head up and standing on tiptoe, she kissed his lips. "Thanks for everything. Good night."

"Good night," he said automatically. "And you're welcome, always. I'll call you tomorrow, okay?"

"Okay." Opening the door, she climbed in, to shut the door and clicked the seatbelt. Starting the car, she drove off, aware that he followed close behind in his Mercedes. Five blocks from her house he turned off and headed home. With a heartfelt sigh, DeAndra continued alone.

At home, she didn't stop to admire her new place or its contemporary furnishings. Dropping her purse on the kitchen counter and her briefcase in a corner, she headed straight for her room, kicking off her shoes. By the time she stretched out on the bed she was crying hard and grabbing a wad of Kleenex from the dispenser on the nightstand.

She'd tried hard to get over her feelings for Damon and although she hadn't succeeded, she'd been okay until he showed up again. She couldn't keep letting him do this to her. There were other people interested in her, plenty of them. If she tried hard, she could learn to love someone else because loving Damon Kessler was a losing proposition.

The burgundy pillowcase was drenched. Turning it over, she let her head sink into the softness.

CHAPTER FOURTEEN

For dinner, Damon found leftover chicken, corn and Brussels sprouts in the refrigerator. Sitting in the kitchen alone, he ate and thought about picking DeAndra up at work and the ride to the repair facility. She'd been pretty animated until they began to talk about their relationship now and in the past. She'd lost that animation and grown more silent after he'd honestly answered her question about marriage.

Sensing that he was treading on dangerous ground, he'd glanced at her repeatedly, to make sure she wasn't hurt. She hadn't given that impression at all, but now that he'd had time to think about it, he was sure he'd managed to hurt her feelings. The thought was like a heavy weight, bringing his spirits down. Remembering the hug and kiss she'd given him at the shop, he realized that her actions had seemed more like a goodbye than a good night.

He stared at the phone, ready to call and apologize. However, experience had taught him to give the situation more time. He'd said he'd call tomorrow. The best thing to do was wait until then. He couldn't bear to think that he'd hurt DeAndra again.

The solitude he'd rejoiced in when he'd first arrived at Cotter's house now seemed oppressive. With the night stretching ahead and nothing but time on his hands, he called Clay at home, talked briefly with Clay's wife, Frenchie, and discovered that Dennis was doing well and scheduled to be released from the hospital. "He sends his thanks for the flowers," Clay added.

"He's welcome, anytime." Damon walked to the sink to rinse his dirty plate, fork, and glass. "Any news on the stalker?"

Clay hesitated. "Don't get upset, but you got a letter yesterday, gloating about the incident in the park and promising more if you don't do right by her."

"I wish I knew who it was so you could lock her up," Damon said in exasperation as he put the dishes in the dishwasher. "I can't lay low in Chicago forever."

Clay's voice rang with authority. "No, but it shouldn't be too long before we figure out who it is. Even though the letters haven't had stamps, we checked the mailbag before the mailman got to the building, just in case someone had slipped it in, but the letter wasn't in it. It seems likely that it came from one of the other offices."

"What?" Damon went back to the table and sat down. "It sounds like the stalker could be someone I know."

"That could very well be. Now don't get too excited. We're handling this and I'm hoping to have things wrapped up by the weekend."

Damon sighed. "I'm looking forward to it."

"How are you and DeAndra doing?"

"I messed up," Damon admitted. "I gave her a big dose of the truth and I think I hurt her feelings."

"What is the truth, man?" Clay asked.

Damon smoothed a hand over the stubble of his beard and mustache. "The truth is that I went through the wringer with Imani and now that I'm learning to enjoy myself again, marriage is not on my agenda."

"Oh man! Oh man!" Clay's voice rose in volume. "You rubbed her nose in that one. You know most of the decent women want to get married, especially if they're fooling around with you between the sheets."

"I never made any promises," Damon said, his voice rising with the injustice of it all, "and the last thing I want to do is take advantage of DeAndra." He'd already spent time on that guilt trip and didn't intend to return. He could hear Clay's wife, Frenchie, adding her two cents in the background.

"Frenchie says you've got to apologize," Clay said.

Damon forced the air from his nose. "I've already figured that out, thank you, but other than hurting her feelings, what am I apologizing for? I don't think I could ever let myself love someone the way I loved Imani, ever again. I simply told her the truth."

"Just do it," Clay directed. "As a married man of six years, I'll tell you that apologies smooth the way and get you out of the doghouse most of the time."

Damon decided that he'd had enough advice for the night. He wanted to end the call. "All right, man, I'll see what I can do. Give me a call if anything breaks loose on the stalker, will you?" With Clay's agreement, he said his goodbyes and hung up the phone.

Taking a quick shower and getting ready for bed, he donned pajamas and took a seat in the recliner with a glass of milk and a copy of *The New York Times* and *The Chicago Tribune*. For background noise, he switched on the television news. Reading the newspapers and halfway listening to the news, he also dozed off a few times. He was dozing lightly when the news reporter got his attention:

"Police and the FBI are closing in on the whereabouts of a missing ten-year-old Chicago girl. Michelle Brown disappeared days ago after receiving a severe beating at the hands of her uncle. She was spotted at a bus station in Nashville, Tennessee, earlier today. Police are following up on the lead. A private donor has offered two thousand dollars for information leading to her safe return. Elsewhere in the news…"

Damon sat up, suddenly wide-awake. Noting the time at the bottom of the screen, he saw that it was close to ten-thirty. Lifting the cordless phone, he didn't hesitate to dial DeAndra's number.

"Hello?" Her voice sounded hoarse and sleepy.

He felt guilty for waking her, but eased it by telling himself that she would soon be thanking him. "DeAndra, it's Damon. Turn on your television and put it on Channel Nine."

"Damon, what's going on?" It was almost a whisper.

"It's about Mouse, so hurry up! I've already seen the piece on the ten o'clock news," he said, his mind conjuring up pictures of an adorable, sleep-drugged DeAndra in some of the sexy lingerie she liked to wear.

"What?" Her voice sounded far from normal. She cleared her throat and he heard the sudden sound of the television on the other end. "Just *tell* me, Damon; did they find her? Is she all right?"

He filled her in. "She was all right earlier today. She was spotted in a bus station in Nashville, Tennessee, and they're moving in on her location. You know that's one of the stops on the way to Alabama, don't you?"

She cleared her throat again. "I really hadn't thought about it. I guess she really must be trying to reach her grandmother's, huh?"

"It sure looks like it." His gaze went to the television screen where the words 'Missing Child' appeared and a reporter began to talk. "Listen, this is it."

The line went silent except for her breathing on the other end as they listened to the news piece on Mouse.

"I think they're close, real close to finding her." Hope lifted her voice and made it soar. "Damon, thanks for calling me. I appreciate it."

Damon shrugged it off. "You're welcome. I just happened to hear the report on the news and I knew you were worried, so I called you. Are you feeling all right?"

"I'm okay. Why?" A testy note had crept into her voice.

"You just sound sort of hoarse, that's all."

"It's my allergies," she said in a tone that precluded any questions.

"Is there anything I can do?" he asked, pushing it.

"No, Damon, I have some pills that I take and then everything goes away."

He decided to go for broke. "DeAndra, if I said anything today or this evening to hurt your feelings, I want to apologize."

"What makes you think you've hurt my feelings?" Her voice reeked with challenge.

Her question threw him so it took a few extra moments more for him to formulate a response. "You changed on me in the car. One minute you were yourself, and the next, you were withdrawn and silent. It was right after I talked about us and said that I was never going to get married."

"What do you want me to say?" Her voice held a poignant quality that went right through him.

Damon smoothed his fingers over the stubble on his face, over and over again. "Just talk to me. Help us solve this issue."

"I don't want you to apologize. I won't accept it because you didn't do anything but tell me how you felt. My hurt feelings don't make it any less valid. Every time I start to dream, you bring me down to earth. You haven't lied to me, Damon, just tried to keep me grounded in reality. I guess it's time I grew up."

Tension tightened the muscles in his neck and his hands balled into fists. He heard the hurt and pain in her voice and he felt responsible, but for the first time in years, he was at a loss for words. "DeAndra…"

Her voice turned brisk. "Good night, Damon."

The line clicked in his ear and he heard the hum of the dial tone. He replaced the receiver, anger, sadness, and righteousness warring inside him. His love for DeAndra might not be the kind of love she wanted, but it was real.

By the time DeAndra got up the next morning, pictures and reports of the police taking Mouse off a bus in Alabama and delivering her to her grandmother were all over the news. There were numerous pictures of the smiling little girl with the fading bruises on her cheek and beneath an eye, not letting the cast and sling on one arm mar her tearful reunion with her grandmother. Apparently, Sonia had agreed that Mouse could stay with her grandmother until things cooled down at home.

DeAndra's heart was full. Happiness at the sight touched her so deeply that she cried. Then she laughed at herself as she went into the bathroom and bathed, dressed, and applied her makeup. It was eight-thirty when she went to work.

"Mr. Sawyer has you down for a nine-thirty appointment," Janice, the main secretary for the associates informed her as she went by. "They're not thinking of firing you, are they?"

DeAndra stopped cold. "I don't think so. I've been holding up my end." Then she remembered that she was supposed to make an appointment to discuss whether her record compared favorably with those of the ones who'd been separated into the group from which junior partners would be chosen. "I guess I'd better get my coffee and get comfortable. See ya later."

"See ya later, and good luck!" the secretary called after her.

Scooting into her office, DeAndra put her purse and suit jacket away. Then she made a quick trip to the Starbucks shop on the first floor of the building and got herself a café latte and a cheese Danish. Back at her desk, she savored the little meal. When she was finished, it was time for her appointment with Sawyer.

Beneath a Picasso painting, Sawyer sat in his luxurious office, looking out at the scenery below. As DeAndra walked in, he smiled and gave her his full attention. She took the seat he indicated at his carved oak conference table, and was surprised when Tina joined them at the last minute, taking the seat across from DeAndra.

"It has come to our attention that you are less than satisfied with the firm's policy of selecting junior partners from a special group of top performers who have been with us for five years or more," Sawyer began in a heavy, formal tone, his hands folded primly on the desk. "Yes, your record of cases won is higher, percentage wise, than the records of some candidates in the select group, but our policy is based on sound judgment and as such, will not change."

Tina leaned forward. "We do value you here, DeAndra, and we want you to stay. We're prepared to offer you a thirty percent pay raise, another salary increase based on your performance in a year, and a free membership in the Executive Bodies Health Club if you will sign an agreement to remain with the firm long enough to be considered for junior partnership."

DeAndra couldn't say a word. Her throat closed with shock. She knew better than to accept their offer on the spot. It would make them think she was easy to pacify and also make them wonder if she had actually been considering another offer. It took two tries to clear her throat. "I'll need time to consider this properly," she managed, proud of the calm, professional sound of her voice.

"Certainly." Tina touched her hand, an expectant expression on her face, "However, we want to be notified if you are seriously considering another offer."

DeAndra nodded. "Of course."

Sawyer's lips formed a straight line. His look of dissatisfaction made her think that he'd been against the firm extending the offer. "You've got a week to make up your mind."

Tina smiled, taking some of the starch out of Sawyer's words. "Is there anything else you'd like to discuss with us?"

It struck DeAndra that though she'd barely had the opportunity to utter a few words, she didn't have the control to continue the talk with them. "No, but I want you to know that I sincerely appreciate the firm making the offer."

Tina nodded. "As I said before, we appreciate you."

Yes! Yes! DeAndra went back to her office with all the dignity and decorum she could muster. Once the door closed behind her, she danced across the floor, shaking her booty, stepping, and prancing as if she'd lost her mind. Really getting into her celebration dance, she even jumped up and down, wiggled, and wound a finger round and round in the air.

By the time she sat down in her desk chair, she was breathing hard. A smile spread across her face as she got back to her caseload. That smile lasted her the rest of the day.

After being out of the office, it felt good to walk out to the parking structure, get into her own car, and drive herself home. This time she let herself into the condo and made herself stop and admire the modern, contemporary look of her kitchen that she'd softened with flowered borders and matching cushions on the chairs.

In the living room, she smoothed her hands across the rich red fabric on the Cameron sofa and the matching, color-coordinated chair. These were things that she'd worked hard to acquire, things that she'd planned and dreamed of owning.

Growing bored with the exercise that usually brought her happiness, DeAndra went back to the kitchen and made grilled chicken and a big fruit salad with pineapple, honeydew, cantaloupe, strawberries, and bananas. Tossing honey and lime over the salad and brushing a little on her chicken, she sat down to eat. The food was good, but she, who liked to be alone, felt lonely.

Finishing her meal, she cleaned up the kitchen and toyed with the idea of going down to the weight room to exercise.

The phone rang. Answering it, she heard the pleasurable sound of Damon's voice. His very essence drew her, even across the phone line.

"So how was your day, DeAndra?" he asked, a warm, caressing note creeping into his voice.

"It was great," she began, excitement bubbling back up to the surface of her thoughts. "Can I get a rerun?" she chuckled. "First there was the news this morning that Mouse is safe and now with her grandmother. When I got to work, I had a meeting with Sawyer and

Hatfield, the two partners you met yesterday. The firm is offering me more money, more money next year based on performance, and a health club membership. They want to know if I'm seriously considering another offer."

Damon spoke from experience. "Of course they do. They've been paying you according to established policies and not making allowances for the quality of your work. DeAndra, you have a very bright future ahead of you."

Lips curving upward with the praise, she said, "Thank you, Damon. I really value your opinion."

"I'm only speaking the truth." His voice rang with conviction. "You were one of the best clerks we ever had. If you ever make it back to the Detroit area, Ramon Richards has said that you've got a standing offer with my old firm. I think you know that."

That threw her, because sometimes she wanted nothing more than to go home where she had family, more friends, and Damon. But she didn't have Damon, did she? He was a popular man and a very eligible bachelor. He would be considered fair game for any woman.

"DeAndra?" His voice cut in on her thoughts.

She responded to his statement, her mind still working with the possibilities. "I'd hoped they would welcome me, but this is the first time I've had it put into words."

"That's because you ran away."

She drew a quick breath. "I didn't run away. I got a job with a prestigious firm in Chicago."

"Yeah, by overlooking what was available to you in Detroit. I'm not proud of the part I may have played in your decision, but it's all in the past. Don't let personal issues sway you from your goals."

Raking her bottom lip with her teeth, she struck back. "I think you might find that bit of advice very useful too, Damon. You're not an old man. Your future should look bright and wonderful, but you've decided to face it alone, just because you happened to fall in love with the wrong woman."

"She wasn't the wrong woman," he said softly. "She just loved Perry more than she loved me."

A sharp thread of emotion cut through her, making her eyelids burn. Damon still loved Imani more than he would ever love her. Her emotions tumbled out in a painful rush. "I know how that feels. When you really love someone and they don't feel the same way, it seems like the pain will never go away."

Swallowing hard, she blinked past the threat of tears. She wasn't going to cry about this today. Too many good things had happened.

"I get the point." Damon's voice was low. "I've told myself the same thing, several times, but the reality is that I'm not ready."

Sensing defeat in his words, she pressed. "But you can't just throw up your hands and go hide in a corner, because this is your life we're talking about. Every day is precious."

"Life is precious," he said, throwing an endpoint on the conversation and letting its weight hold the silence for several moments. "Believe it or not, I really called to ask you to dinner. Do you think you'd like to go to dinner with a friend who's been hiding in a corner?"

"I've already had dinner," she told him, remembering all the times when she would have gone along anyway. She needed to stay home and get her head straight. If she continued to see Damon, she had to accept the way things were. She didn't think she could do it.

"Maybe we could do something tomorrow?" he asked, a hopeful note in his voice.

"Tomorrow's girls' night out. Maybe sometime this weekend?" she suggested, not quite wanting to give up yet. Maybe she would have it all straight in her mind by then.

"You're not dumping me because of the marriage issue, are you?"

His frank question startled her. How can you dump someone you really haven't been together with? "I-I really don't know how you feel about us having been together, Damon. It meant a lot to me, but som people would just consider it sleeping together."

"DeAndra, it meant a lot to me too. I sorry if I didn't make it perfectly clear. I'm not one to casually sleep around. You've known me long enough to know that."

She nodded, her breath coming out in a sigh. "Yes, but it's good to hear the words anyway." She'd met several of Damon's girlfriends and only a few had been astute enough to see her as a threat. Many of them he'd simply dated. He'd been very selective about the women he slept with.

"I'll call you about this weekend," he said, his disappointment evident. "Take care, DeAndra, I'll be seeing you."

"Good night," she answered, and hung up the phone. Her thoughts ping-ponged back and forth. Was she crazy not to snatch every possible minute with Damon? The stalker situation couldn't drag on much longer. And what would she do when he left?

Finally, she settled on the couch with a copy of the latest Genesis romance.

Damon hung up the phone, at a loss for fixing things. He'd known DeAndra longer than any of the other women he'd dated. They had a lot of history. Why did he suddenly have such a hard time communicating with her? Hopefully she hadn't given up on him because he wanted her in his life. Grabbing his keys, he decided to treat himself to a meal at the Cheesecake Factory.

Waiting alone for a table at the restaurant, he was amazed at the number of women who approached him and found time to chat. A few offered to eat dinner with him, doing wonders for his ego, but Damon declined. DeAndra was the only woman with whom he wanted to have dinner.

CHAPTER FIFTEEN

The next evening, DeAndra found a short, tight little gold dress and matching three-inch heels to wear for her night out with the girls. They'd all agreed to dress 'hot.' Staring at herself in the mirror, she wondered if this was going a little too far. She looked ready for action. Her friends were looking for action, but deep inside DeAndra only wanted to hang with the girls and then she wanted to go home to Damon. *No chance of that happening!*

They'd all chipped in to pay her friend Macy's brother to chauffer them around from club to club in an elegant black limousine. For once, each of the friends was between boyfriends and ready to party.

As DeAndra added diamond stud earrings, the phone rang. Answering, she was surprised to hear the excited, high-pitched voice on the other end. "Mouse!"

"Hi Ms. Blake! Grandma said you were worried about me."

"I was. Are you all right now?"

"Yes."

DeAndra pictured her little friend on the other end of the line, two thick braids bobbing every time she moved her head, and her brown eyes sparkling. "What about your arm? When I saw you on TV you had it in a sling."

"It only hurts a little. Grandma took me to the doctor and got some medicine. I like staying with Grandma. Mama says I can stay until September."

"I'm going to miss you, honey."

"I'm going to miss you too, Ms. Blake, and all my friends, and the people at the center."

DeAndra chose that moment to ask a question that had been on her mind since hearing of Mouse being sighted at the bus station. "Mouse, where did you get the money for the bus?"

"Rico took a collection from all our friends and added his allowance money. I had some too," she added proudly. "I didn't have enough to eat with, but people kept giving me food and money."

"You really should not accept anything from strangers," DeAndra cautioned her.

The little girl's voice turned sheepish. "I know, Grandma was mad about that, but I was hungry. Nobody hurt me and everybody was nice."

"If you do it again, you might not be so lucky," DeAndra couldn't help adding. "I don't really want to lecture you, but we were *so* worried."

"But I'm okay now, Ms. Blake. Uncle Eric is in jail and I'm safe with my grandma."

DeAndra words came with heavy emphasis. "Yes, you are, honey, and I am so relieved! You take care of yourself, okay?"

"Yes."

"And ask Grandma to let you call me every once in a while. You can call collect."

"Thanks, Ms. Blake. I love you."

"Love you too." Replacing the receiver, DeAndra felt the smile right down to her bones. *Thank you, God.*

Damon spent most of Friday working hard on his cases, checking references, precedents, and pondering the rules of law. When evening came, he stopped to call Clay for progress on his case. This time his friend was extraordinarily tight-lipped about the activities in Detroit. He would only say that he still believed that Damon's stalker worked in the building where his office was and that he was gathering evidence against a number of suspects. When the subject of DeAndra came up, Damon took a turn at being close-mouthed. Taking leave of each other, the two friends ended the call.

The notion of his stalker being someone in his downtown office building stayed with Damon long after the call. He tried to remember people and incidences where he'd received undue attention and drew a blank. Frustrated, he used some of his energy to fix a dinner of spaghetti and chicken parmesan with Italian stir-fried vegetables.

Alone, he sat at the table and savored every scrumptious bit of his food with a glass of merlot. He spared a number of thoughts for DeAndra, who was probably spending big bucks for lesser fare and fancy drinks.

Tired from his day, he went to bed early, thinking about DeAndra.

On Saturday he got up early, his mind clear and focused as he showered, dressed in a casual shirt and pants, and made breakfast. In bright, early morning sunlight, he ate scrambled eggs with cheese and bacon, and a couple of slices of wheat toast.

As he drank his coffee in Cotter's office area, he typed in the name of the legal center where DeAndra volunteered every other weekend. The street address came up right away. A grin lit his face as he clicked on the printer. He planned to surprise DeAndra and he didn't plan to go away until everything was settled between them.

Cleaning the place took an hour and a half. Then Damon took his car to the hand car wash and waited his turn for service. The crew did a magnificent job. The icing on the cake came when he still arrived at the center just in time to see DeAndra walking in. *Good timing!*

Glad she hadn't seen him yet, Damon parked his car close to DeAndra's, just noticing that a small group of people stood just across the street with protest signs. Mildly curious, he tilted his head, trying to read some of the signs, and failed. Noting that the street was otherwise deserted, he followed DeAndra into the building with the thought that he would not stay for long.

A security guard met him just inside the entrance. "I'm sorry sir, but there's no service here until ten o'clock."

Damon checked his watch. He had at least fifteen minutes. "I'm a personal friend of Ms. Blake's," he said, walking down the long row of empty chairs as if he'd already been granted permission.

The guard followed close behind him until they reached a large room with four office cubicles separated by large orange partitions. Front and center, looking wonderful in a short, wine-colored suit that showed off her fabulous legs, DeAndra stood pulling a stack of files from an old cabinet. She turned as he halted at the doorway, surprised but with welcome in her eyes. "Damon! What are you doing here?"

"I thought we should talk." Damon moved closer.

"Ms. Blake, he said he was a friend of yours," the guard said belatedly.

She nodded. "He is, George. It's okay."

As the guard walked back to his station, Damon stepped into the room and pulled the door shut.

Her eyes widened as he approached. "Wh-what did you want to say?"

Damon reached her and his hands cupping her delicate face, tilting it up. The fresh fruity scent of her shampoo mixed with the hint of sandalwood in her cologne and filled his nostrils. "This." His mouth came down on hers, relishing the delicious taste of her mouth, his tongue circling and sliding against hers with a fevered passion that made them both groan.

He felt her small hands at his waist, pulling him closer as he slid restless hands down her back to cup her hips. "I missed you," he whispered, stopping to simply hold her.

"I missed you too." She laid her head against his chest.

He folded her in closer, stroking her soft curls. "And I thought you were out getting a replacement."

She blew against his chest, her hot breath hardening the points of his nipples. "You're not that easy to replace. Besides, I don't want to do that. I thought about you all night long."

"Me too." He pulled back to look into her big brown eyes. "So what are we going to do about it?"

She let him back her into the desk and then lift her up and set her on top of it. Massaging his hands up her nylon-clad legs, he caressed the bare skin at the top of her stockings. Pushing her short skirt higher, he stepped into the cradle of her thighs.

"Damon." Leaning forward, she trailed her hands down his chest to his waist. "I'd like to say anytime, anywhere, but you know, I've never, ever fantasized about making love here."

Glancing around the room, he took in the deep beige walls, old wood and chrome desks, and orange partitions. "I can see why."

Heat sizzled between them as they gazed into each other's eyes, considering the proposition.

A loud rapping on the door interrupted them. "Ms. Blake? Ms. Blake, you in there?" an elderly female voice inquired.

Reining himself in, Damon stepped back, watching her sensual movement as she jumped down from the desk, pulling down her skirt. "I can come back later," he offered, "take you to lunch or dinner."

"Stay. We need all the help we can get." Placing her hands over her face, she closed her eyes for a few moments. When she opened them again, her professional persona was in place.

The knocking started again, the same voice calling out.

"I'll be right out," DeAndra called in a cool voice. "Staying?" she asked Damon, a challenge in her eyes. "I know that you're not licensed to practice in Illinois, but there is still a lot you could do. You could help with the paperwork and separate the types of cases outside so that I can make sure every client gets helped today."

Walking to the door and throwing it open, she revealed several people occupying chairs in the hall. "I believe you're first," she told the eld erly woman who had vacated the first chair to knock on the door.

"Yes, I am, chile." Using her walker, the woman entered the room and took a seat in the chair in front of DeAndra's desk.

DeAndra threw him a glance and he made up his mind. They obviously needed help and even though his options were limited, he could help. "I'm staying," he said, drawing up a chair.

DeAndra made quick introductions and they got down to business. After a while, Damon went out to the hall and interviewed clients, one by one, helping them with the required paperwork and setting them up for DeAndra.

When it was time for lunch, they headed for the car, only to find the street crowded with police, protesters, and some television news crews.

"What's up with that?" Damon asked, eyeing the crowd.

"A fourteen-year-old got killed in an incident with an off duty police officer and everyone is upset about it," DeAndra said, standing just outside the center with him.

"We'll have to take a rain check on lunch." Damon ducked back into the building, "The last thing I want is to appear on television."

Back against the door, she grinned. "We can share the lunch I brought before I knew you were coming to take me away from it all."

Turning, Damon walked her back down the hall. "What do you have?"

"PB&J, a banana, a peach, bag of chips, and a bottle of Sprite Remix."

Damon wrinkled his nose. "Peanut butter and jelly? I haven't had that since I was a kid!"

"Okay, then you can have the peach and the banana," DeAndra said smoothly.

"No," Damon protested. "I still want half of the PB&J. I need my protein."

"We'll start seeing clients again at one," DeAndra announced as they passed several potential clients still lining the halls in the old wooden chairs. Then she and Damon went back into the office and shut the door. They were alone in the room.

Damon spread the desk with newspaper and DeAndra added a covering of paper towels.

As she spread her lunch out on the desktop, Damon asked, "Do you want to talk now?"

She scanned him, reticence in her brown eyes. "No, I don't want to be serious right now. I want to enjoy you being here, having lunch with me."

Her words flattered and pulled at him. He wanted her to be happy. "Okay." He leaned over and kissed her cheek. "So where are we having our picnic?"

"Oh, can't you tell that's Flower Hall over there? We're in Douglas Park."

"Douglas Park." Damon gazed off in the distance as if he could actually see a park around them. "Is that the water over there?"

"Yes." DeAndra gave him half the sandwich and placed the bottle of pop in the center of the table. "Come on, sit down."

Damon dropped down into a chair and they began to eat. When they were done, they moved their chairs together, held hands, and kissed. When it was time to start work again, they separated reluctantly and got busy.

After a particularly difficult day, Chief Clay got home a couple of hours early and found sanctuary on the couch, in front of the television. He sipped a beer and watched the news while he waited for his wife to finish preparing dinner. The news anchor talked about a large angry demonstration that had been staged in Chicago because a kid had died after being shot by an off duty police officer. A few people in the crowd were interviewed and then the camera panned the area.

One thing that really got Clay's attention was the yellow Mercedes parked across the street from the demonstration. In one of the shots, he stopped the frame with his satellite recorder system and could even make out the first three letters on the license plate, "JDK."

Clay shot up from the couch, reaching for the phone and fuming. He'd told Damon to stay out of the limelight. Anybody who knew Damon knew that yellow Mercedes and his license plate with initials for Judge Damon Kessler. As the phone rang again and again, Clay wondered if anyone else had seen Damon's car. If his stalker had been watching, this was tantamount to an invitation. When the voice mail came on, Clay hung up in frustration. He decided to wait ten minutes and then call again.

Ten minutes later, he dialed again and got the voice mail. "Damon, if you've still got your car parked across from that demonstration, you need to move it right away. Your stalker may know where you are. Call me when you get this message."

Damon and DeAndra headed for the door. It had been a long day, but being together had changed everything, making it enjoyable. As they made it to the entrance, DeAndra looked out at their cars and the area across the street. "The protesters are gone."

"I'm glad to hear that." Damon did a double-check as a single car went by. Then he opened the door for her.

Thanking him, she stepped out into the warm evening air. "Want to go to dinner?"

"Sure. We can go in my car and come back for yours." Damon followed her out, carrying her briefcase.

They walked a little slowly, drinking in the warm sunshine and sounds of birds and children at play.

"Where do you want to go?" Damon asked as they reached the car and he opened the passenger door.

"Shaw's Crab House?" she asked, folding herself into the car and clicking the seat belt.

"Mmmm, I like that idea." Matching her smile, he slammed the door shut and started the walk around to the driver's side of the car.

The air suddenly exploded with a loud, popping noise just as he rounded the rear of the car. Damon jumped, turning at the sound of a projectile slamming into the sidewalk. *Was that a gunshot? It had to be!* His head whipped one way and then the other, looking someone with a gun. He saw no one.

Racing along the left side in what seemed like slow motion, he heard a woman screaming his name. A rushing sound and the frantic pounding of his heart filled his ears. Again the air exploded, but this time something hot slammed into his left arm, knocking him off balance. Damon stumbled, pain and agony erupting and spreading through his entire arm. *Dear God, I'm not going to make it. I'm going to be shot down in the street like a dog!*

He held on to his keys, his and DeAndra's only hope was to escape in the car. Catching himself with legs conditioned from several hours a week spent running, he regained his balance and turned his body so that he could lift his uninjured right arm and pull on the driver's door. On its own, it came open slowly. Damon stepped back out of its path. He saw DeAndra, crouching low on the seat and working the door, desperately calling to him.

He hated that he'd brought his trouble to her. He rushed forward towards the relative safety of the car door. Abruptly, another bullet smashed into his side, searing it with burning fire. Damon went down in the street, writhing under the lash of excruciating pain. He couldn't move. Warm blood soaked his shirt.

He must have lost a few minutes. Disoriented, he opened his eyes and saw DeAndra, exposed to the shooter as she crouched in the open car door, pulling at him, crying his name hysterically, urging him to move and demanding it. It took some time, but he began to inch his body forward.

The door opened wider as DeAndra tried to help him into the car.

"Keys. Take the keys," he urged, unwilling to take comfort in the fact that the shooting seemed to have stopped.

Her fingers closed on him and the keys. "Get in Damon. I'll drive."

Gratefully gaining the driver's seat, he tried in vain to maneuver himself over to the other side. There was blood everywhere. He couldn't make his body move the way he needed it to. Damon fell back against the seat. "I-I can't."

"Move over Damon!" Leaning in to insert the keys in the ignition, she switched it on. "I'm going to squeeze in with you and it's going to hurt, but we've got to get out of here." She pressed in against him, trying to fit into the small space.

Gasping, Damon bit back curses as he grunted with pain. A last bullet ripped through the driver's side window. He heard DeAndra cry out, then a heavy falling sound. She was no longer in the car.

"DeAndra?" he called, "DeAndra!" No answer. A deep, numbing paralysis captured his throat and chest. A shocking vision formed in his mind of her lying on the ground beside the car, dead of a wound to the head. Forcing that image from his mind, Damon lay on the seat, unable to move. He heard sirens in the distance. He prayed that help would make it in time.

"DeAndra?" he called out, "Baby please say something. Don't leave me like this. Tell me you're okay." The answering silence was more eloquent than any words. DeAndra was gone and he would never have another chance to love her and let her know how he really felt. His world was crashing down around him. Damon choked out an agonized cry. "DeAndra!"

CHAPTER SIXTEEN

Damon floated on a soft fluffy cloud of nothingness where pain did not exist. He saw, heard, and felt nothing. Gradually he tired of this particular existence and pushed toward consciousness of the muffled pain in his body, the things around him and memories of what had happened.

Shivering, he felt cold, and he couldn't make his body move the way he wanted it to. His left arm was still and immobile. A great swath of tight bandaging covered his midsection. His body still ached beneath it with a dull pain.

Someone drew warm blankets up to cover him. "DeAndra?"

"She's not here," a crisp woman's voice replied.

Damon pried his lids open, blinking against the bright, glaring light in the white hospital room. They snapped shut tightly, burning.

"Let me turn off the lights." With a rustling sound, the woman moved around the room, clicking off lights.

When all went silent, Damon tried again, opening his eyes to gray daylight filtering in from a window. He blinked, noting that his room was private and his nurse, a tall, dark-haired, efficient-looking woman, stood close to the bed.

"Feeling better?" she asked, adjusting the IV in his arm.

"Where is DeAndra?" he asked, praying that she hadn't died in the street, right by his car. It seemed that he had been calling to her forever and she had never answered.

"You've been calling for her," the nurse observed, "so when I heard that they'd brought you in with a young woman, I checked on her too. She's still here, and her condition is stable, but she's not able to visi you."

Damon's breath released on a long sigh and the pressure in his head eased. He wouldn't have been able to accept DeAndra's death. His thoughts returned to their imaginary lunch in the park and the fun and camaraderie they'd enjoyed before it all came crashing down. He felt guilty that he'd somehow brought the stalker down on DeAndra. "When can I see her?" he asked, needing to see her face before he could let himself totally relax.

"Ah, I'll have to check. She's in a—a different section of the hospital."

"What's wrong with her?" Damon asked, picking up a hesitancy in the nurse's speech. Memories of the sound of the bullet smashing through the window and the heavy sound of a body falling flooded his thoughts. His hands made fists beneath the blankets.

"Specifics on Ms. Blake's condition are private information, Mr. Kessler, unless of course, you're a family member?"

"No, but I am a friend of the family," he said, grasping at straws.

"Well, I have a friend who works in that area. I'll see if she can get you the name of one of the family members when they visit."

"Thank you." Damon closed his eyes, wondering about the type of reception he would get from DeAndra's family. Everything had been great until he'd gotten himself engaged to Imani.

"Mr. Kessler? We still need to talk about you," the nurse insisted, lifting his chart from the stand to scan it. "Any pain?"

"No."

"We took a bullet from your side. You were lucky that it missed your kidneys. We took another out of your arm. There may be some nerve damage there."

Damon nodded, his head sinking into the pillow. "Did they catch the shooter?"

"Not yet." Her facial expression turned sympathetic, "But don't worry, Mr. Kessler, the police have guards stationed outside and both your and Ms. Blake's rooms."

"Thank God for that." Closing his eyes, Damon rested, his mind already at work on getting in to see DeAndra.

Damon awakened to find Warfield Clay sitting in the chair by the bed. "Clay! It's good to see you, man! For a while I thought it was all over for me and DeAndra."

Clay pushed his chair closer. "You don't know how good it feels to see you're still alive and kicking, ol' buddy!" He grabbed Damon's good hand in one of his and patted it. "It feels even better to sit here knowing we've got your stalker."

"You do?" Damon resisted the urge to sit up. He wasn't feeling that good and it was about time for more pain medication. "Who was it? Anybody I know?"

Clay nodded. "Yes, I'm sorry to say. Remember your secretary's friend?"

"*Rachel?*" The name came out Damon's mouth, but he didn't see how that painfully shy young lady could be his stalker and he told Clay so.

"You see ol' man, we got a little suspicious when your secretary had to spend a lot of time thinking up things to tell her friend when you dropped out of sight. Other people were very interested too, but dear Rachel had unparalleled access to your office and your secretary. Apparently, she was good at distracting Tori when she wanted to leave those letters. Then she took time off from work after you graciously left your car in sight of a television crew," he said, giving Damon the how-could-you-be-so-stupid look, "and someone showed up in Chicago to use you and Ms. Blake as shooting targets."

Damon stared at his friend, shaking his head in disbelief. "Yeah, but…"

On a roll, Clay pressed on. "Before I had a crew come in to clean up the mess she made of your house, we checked everywhere for evidence. Can you believe that we found shoes in her closet, same size and make to match a dirty print we found in your bathroom? We found the gun used to shoot you and Ms. Blake in a phony book she kept in her bookcase, and we found her fingerprints on it."

Damon forced the breath from his lungs. "But why, man? She seemed like a sweet kid."

"And was nuttier than a fruitcake," Clay added with conviction. "She's seeing a shrink and has been in and out of mental hospitals due to her inability to cope with her traumatic childhood."

Dazed, Damon lay there replaying the times he'd seen Rachel in the office and the conversations they'd had. He'd never have believed it in a million years.

Clay interrupted his thoughts. "Hey ol' man, I'd have brought you a fruit basket, but they said you're not on solid food yet."

"Yeah, breakfast was that soft egg mess, chicken broth, and tea. The funny thing is that even though I complained, I had a hard enough time getting that down."

"The flowers up there are from me, Frenchie, and Dennis," Clay said, pointing to a bouquet of flowers that included everything roses, lilies, and chrysanthemums.

Turning his head to thank Clay, Damon inhaled their fragrance. It drew his thoughts back to DeAndra. "Did you stop to see DeAndra too?" he asked Clay.

Clay flashed him a sympathetic look. "No, but I checked into her condition, and even though she's still unconscious, she's stable."

This time Damon did try to sit up. He fell back against sheets in a haze of pain that he almost welcomed. He couldn't face the thought of DeAndra failing to regain consciousness. All the more damning was the fact that he blamed himself for leading the stalker to her.

"Damon! You know it's too soon for you to be trying to move

around like that!" Clay snapped, eyeing the thick swath of bandages covering Damon's midsection. "I'll ring for your nurse."

Fifteen minutes later Damon was breathing easier. Freshly administered medication had already taken away most of the pain, but Damon could not rest. He had to see DeAndra for himself. He wouldn't have any sense of peace until he did.

Clay spent the night in a nearby hotel and came back in the morning to visit until it was time to go catch the plane for home. Glad to see his friend again, Damon asked for help in personally checking on DeAndra.

True to his word, Clay commandeered a wheelchair, managed to get a fully medicated Damon into it, and wheeled him down to DeAndra's room.

Her brother Larry and her mother were sitting in the room. An older, harder version of DeAndra, Mrs. Blake looked as if she had been crying.

Larry turned unfriendly eyes upon Damon. "If you'd stayed away from Dee, she'd be okay now."

Damon's heart was heavy in his chest. He couldn't argue with the truth. "I didn't mean to put her in danger," he said, hoarsely. "I love DeAndra. In fact, she had been staying with me because someone else had threatened her."

Mrs. Blake blew her nose. "You know the police told you about that, Larry," she admonished him in a soft voice.

"I don't care! I want you to stay away from my sister. You always find a way to hurt her. She thinks we don't know why she suddenly left Detroit, but we do. It was because of you."

Damon felt himself recoiling from the venom in Larry's words and expression. Since he already felt guilty, he couldn't find the words to defend himself.

"Son, Damon is as much a victim as DeAndra," Clay said, pushing him further into the room, "That should be obvious."

"Larry, wait for me in the hall." Mrs. Blake's voice rang out.

Sparing Damon one last malevolent glare, the boy obeyed sullenly.

When Larry was gone, Mrs. Blake approached Damon. "I know you love DeAndra and that you wouldn't knowingly do anything to hurt her. I'm glad you're here to see her. Talk to her. Maybe she'll answer for you."

Nodding, Damon thanked her, nodding, Damon thanked her, watching as she wiped away a tear.

Clay left him alone with DeAndra.

"DeAndra," he began, taking her limp hand as he focused on her face, "Baby, it's not over yet. I've got a new challenge for you and I know you can do it. I'm here rooting for you. Your mother and Larry are too. We love you, sweetheart. We want to see you smile again and hear you voice. Baby you're too precious to slip away from us..."

She never moved. Damon stayed for hours, holding her small, limp hand in his and just looking at her. It wasn't much, but just being with her lifted his spirits and gave him hope.

She lay on her back with her eyes closed, as if she were only sleeping. Damon knew better. He'd talked to the nurse and discovered that she was still unconscious. She'd been winged by the bullet that smashed through the car window and then fallen out of the car to hit her head against the pavement. There'd been some swelling in her brain. Looking at the sweet innocence still evident in her beautiful face, he prayed that she would awaken still herself, with all her senses.

As the week wore on, Damon recovered steadily and was released from the hospital, but DeAndra's condition remained a concern. Her wounds were healing and the swelling went down, but she remained unconscious. He spent long hours at her side, talking to her.

The day after he was released, Damon sat in the chair by her bed, holding her hand and watching the play of sunlight on her face. His fingers lost themselves in her soft curls and moved on to trace the delicate curve of her cheek. It really hurt to see her like this.

Swallowing hard, he grasped her hand tightly and leaned forward to kiss her cheek. He felt her cheek move beneath his lips. Jerking back, he studied her. "DeAndra?"

Her open mouth formed words that weren't quite whispers.

"I can't hear you, sweetheart," Damon told her, caressing her hand with both of his. "Try harder."

Her lashes fluttered and opened in the dim light. "Damon."

Thank you, God. He covered her face with reverent kisses. "You came back."

Her voice was hoarse with disuse. "Yes, Damon. I came back for you." She touched his face, wondering at the moisture glistening in his eyes. Damon had tears—for her!

"I really love you, you know that?" he stammered.

"I love you too, Damon." Her throat threatened to close. Somehow Damon figured it out and put a straw in her mouth. She took a few small sips of cool water. Then he replaced it on her bedside table.

"I mean that I really, really love you. You can't know how hard it was to sit in this chair and look at you, and know that you might never say my name again. I talked to you for hours on end and you couldn't answer." He gently drew her into his arms. "Do you think you could reconsider a job in Detroit?"

"Why?" She felt disoriented from all the movement, but was determined to enjoy being in Damon's arms.

"Because I've fallen in love with you. I can't stand the thought of us being apart. Yes, I've loved you for years and years, but I didn't understand how strong and deep it was. I need to share it and my life with you. Will you marry me?"

"Damon!" Her head spun for several reasons, but she held on to Damon.

"Say yes, sweetheart, you're making me nervous."

"Yes, Damon, I'll marry you, and we'll figure out the living situation." Tears slipped down her face.

"Yes, but being apart is not one of the options." Damon kissed her lips. "Why are you crying?"

"I didn't think you'd ever get around to asking me," she confided.

Damon chuckled. "Then I guess we're even on that one. I was afraid that I wouldn't get the chance. I almost lost you."

Holding each other close, they promised to love each other till the end of time.

AUTHOR BIOGRAPHY

Natalie Dunbar is a Detroit area engineer and University of Michigan graduate who has never been able to resist a good story. From creating plays to perform with her sisters at the age of eight, to writing romantic episodes for Star Trek's Mr. Spock, and finally penning romance novels that encompass all her favorite heroes, she has always enjoyed romance. For Natalie, romantic fiction represents the great escape into the most exciting adventure imaginable: LOVE.

Married to her high school sweetheart, Natalie lives in the Detroit area with her husband and their two boys. *Best of Friends* is her first Indigo love story. Read more about Natalie at www.nataliedunbar.com

EXCERPT FROM

HARD TO LOVE
BY
KIMBERLEY WHITE

"Mia!" Alexandra Bramble jumped from her chair, arms opened wide to greet her only friend.

Fashionably late, Mia sauntered up to the table in the outdoor Paris café. They embraced as women do who have a friendship based more on history than earned trust. Two men left their seats to help the supermodel into her chair. "Merci," Mia thanked them. The ladies watched the men trip over themselves back to their seats.

"Does this happen everywhere you go?" Alexandra asked with a coy smile.

"Everywhere. It's tiresome."

"I don't remember you being so tall."

Mia could stop traffic with her six-foot, perfectly thin body. The fact God had blessed her with a gorgeous face made of pronounced cheekbones, a slender nose, huge eyes and a bow mouth added salt to the wound. As Alexandra ate her lunch without interruption, she couldn't envy Mia's plight. Man after man, American and French, solicited a photo or autograph from her. Her cover on the Sports Illustrated swimsuit issue propelled her to the top of the modeling game. Tyra Banks, Petra and Cathy Ireland wished they could achieve Mia's supermodel status.

Alexandra had achieved a respectable status of her own in the beauty industry when she founded Jhoni Cosmetics, a line of African-American make-up and hair care products. The addition of exotic perfumes helped Jhoni corner the market. At thirty, she was wealthy beyond her dreams.

She considered her good looks a curse because men didn't take her seriously in the corporate world. They stared at her long, shapely legs or watched her lips with dreamy fascination when they should have been listening to her promotional plans. They asked her out for long weekends on private islands when they should have been inviting her to board meetings. They whistled when she walked by instead of jumping out of her way. They feared she wouldn't offer them a night in her bed when they should have worried she would crush them with her business savvy.

"Let me be the first to congratulate you," Mia said once the last wave of adoring fans left her to eat her lunch.

"Condolences might be more in order." Perturbed, Alexandra ripped at her croissant.

"The meeting didn't go as planned?"

"Not at all. Jhoni didn't win the contract."

"Don't worry," Mia said in a wispy voice, "there will be others." She never had a care in the world. There were people in Mia's entourage responsible for shouldering her burdens. Wouldn't want to stress the supermodel, the fear of worry-lines and all. For all the years Alexandra had known Mia, she always seemed to have her head in the clouds. Nothing bothered her. She believed everything would turn out right. Alexandra envied her naïveté.

"It's not that simple, Mia. Without this contract Jhoni is in trouble." Like most companies in the United States, Jhoni was suffering recent economic hardship. This was the time to do or die, sink or swim. Stable companies with solid financial plans who adapted quickly to the recession would survive. The others would fade away. Alexandra could not let Jhoni fold. She would not go back to the way life had been before she had money to buy anything she wanted.

Explaining all this to Mia proved difficult, but once she understood she sympathized with Alexandra. "What can I do to help?"

"I have a two-part plan." Alexandra watched Mia spear a leaf of lettuce and dunk it in low calorie dressing. Once she had her attention again, she continued. "Jhoni would like to hire you to promote our make-up line. I know I should go through your agent, but this is too important to me to get weighed down with attorneys and accountants."

"No problem."

Just like that, easy. "I'm talking commercials and print ads."

"No problem. I'll have my agent call you to book the dates."

"I'll offer a fair contract, but I can't pay what you're used to making."

Mia waved away her worry. "I don't have a head for business. You'll talk with my agent and work it out. If he's unreasonable, call me." Everything came easy for Mia. "I miss the States. I miss home. Tell me what everyone in our set is doing."

"I'd hoped we could catch up on the plane."

Mia shook her head. "Sorry. I have a show this weekend in Nigeria."

"Nigeria? Is there anywhere on the globe you haven't been?"

Mia thought for a long moment. "I don't suppose there is."

2005 Publication Schedule

January

A Heart's Awakening
Veronica Parker
$9.95
1-58571-143-9

Falling
Natalie Dunbar
$9.95
1-58571-121-7

February

Echoes of Yesterday
Beverly Clark
$9.95
1-58571-131-4

A Love of Her Own
Cheris F. Hodges
$9.95
1-58571-136-5

Higher Ground
Leah Latimer
$19.95
1-58571-157-8

March

Misconceptions
Pamela Leigh Starr
$9.95
1-58571-117-9

I'll Paint a Sun
Al Garotto
$9.95
1-58571-165-9

Peace Be Still
Colette Haywood
$12.95
1-58571-129-2

April

Intentional Mistakes
Michele Sudler
$9.95
1-58571-152-7

Conquering Dr. Wexler's Heart
Kimberley White
$9.95
1-58571-126-8

Song in the Park
Martin Brant
$15.95
1-58571-125-X

May

The Color Line
Lizette Carter
$9.95
1-58571-163-2

Unconditional
A.C. Arthur
$9.95
1-58571-142-X

Last Train to Memphis
Elsa Cook
$12.95
1-58571-146-2

June

Angel's Paradise
Janice Angelique
$9.95
1-58571-107-1

Suddenly You
Crystal Hubbard
$9.95
1-58571-158-6

Matters of Life and Death
Lesego Malepe, Ph.D.
$15.95
1-58571-124-1

2005 Publication Schedule (continued)

July

Pleasures All Mine
Belinda O. Steward
$9.95
1-58571-112-8

Wild Ravens
Altonya Washington
$9.95
1-58571-164-0

Class Reunion
Irma Jenkins/John Brown
$12.95
1-58571-123-3

August

Path of Thorns
Annetta P. Lee
$9.95
1-58571-145-4

Timeless Devotion
Bella McFarland
$9.95
1-58571-148-9

Life Is Never As It Seems
June Michael
$12.95
1-58571-153-5

September

Beyond the Rapture
Beverly Clark
$9.95
1-58571-131-4

Blood Lust
J. M. Jeffries
$9.95
1-58571-138-1

Rough on Rats and Tough
on Cats
Chris Parker
$12.95
1-58571-154-3

October

A Will to Love
Angie Daniels
$9.95
1-58571-141-1

Taken by You
Dorothy Elizabeth Love
$9.95
1-58571-162-4

Soul Eyes
Wayne L. Wilson
$12.95
1-58571-147-0

November

A Drummer's Beat to
Mend
Kay Swanson
$9.95

Sweet Reprecussions
Kimberley White
$9.95
1-58571-159-4

Red Polka Dot in a
Worldof Plaid
Varian Johnson
$12.95
1-58571-140-3

December

Hand in Glove
Andrea Jackson
$9.95
1-58571-166-7

Blaze
Barbara Keaton
$9.95

Across
Carol Payne
$12.95
1-58571-149-7

Other Genesis Press, Inc. Titles

Acquisitions	Kimberley White	$8.95
A Dangerous Deception	J.M. Jeffries	$8.95
A Dangerous Love	J.M. Jeffries	$8.95
A Dangerous Obsession	J.M. Jeffries	$8.95
After the Vows	Leslie Esdaile	$10.95
(Summer Anthology)	T.T. Henderson	
	Jacqueline Thomas	
Again My Love	Kayla Perrin	$10.95
Against the Wind	Gwynne Forster	$8.95
A Lark on the Wing	Phyliss Hamilton	$8.95
A Lighter Shade of Brown	Vicki Andrews	$8.95
All I Ask	Barbara Keaton	$8.95
A Love to Cherish	Beverly Clark	$8.95
Ambrosia	T.T. Henderson	$8.95
And Then Came You	Dorothy Elizabeth Love	$8.95
Angel's Paradise	Janice Angelique	$8.95
A Risk of Rain	Dar Tomlinson	$8.95
At Last	Lisa G. Riley	$8.95
Best of Friends	Natalie Dunbar	$8.95
Bound by Love	Beverly Clark	$8.95
Breeze	Robin Hampton Allen	$10.95
Brown Sugar Diaries &	Delores Bundy &	$10.95
Other Sexy Tales	Cole Riley	
By Design	Barbara Keaton	$8.95
Cajun Heat	Charlene Berry	$8.95
Careless Whispers	Rochelle Alers	$8.95
Caught in a Trap	Andre Michelle	$8.95
Chances	Pamela Leigh Starr	$8.95
Dark Embrace	Crystal Wilson Harris	$8.95
Dark Storm Rising	Chinelu Moore	$10.95
Designer Passion	Dar Tomlinson	$8.95
Ebony Butterfly II	Delilah Dawson	$14.95
Erotic Anthology	Assorted	$8.95
Eve's Prescription	Edwina Martin Arnold	$8.95
Everlastin' Love	Gay G. Gunn	$8.95

Fate	Pamela Leigh Starr	$8.95
Forbidden Quest	Dar Tomlinson	$10.95
Fragment in the Sand	Annetta P. Lee	$8.95
From the Ashes	Kathleen Suzanne	$8.95
	Jeanne Sumerix	
Gentle Yearning	Rochelle Alers	$10.95
Glory of Love	Sinclair LeBeau	$10.95
Hart & Soul	Angie Daniels	$8.95
Heartbeat	Stephanie Bedwell-Grime	$8.95
I'll Be Your Shelter	Giselle Carmichael	$8.95
Illusions	Pamela Leigh Starr	$8.95
Indiscretions	Donna Hill	$8.95
Interlude	Donna Hill	$8.95
Intimate Intentions	Angie Daniels	$8.95
Just an Affair	Eugenia O'Neal	$8.95
Kiss or Keep	Debra Phillips	$8.95
Love Always	Mildred E. Riley	$10.95
Love Unveiled	Gloria Greene	$10.95
Love's Deception	Charlene Berry	$10.95
Mae's Promise	Melody Walcott	$8.95
Meant to Be	Jeanne Sumerix	$8.95
Midnight Clear	Leslie Esdaile	$10.95
(Anthology)	Gwynne Forster	
	Carmen Green	
	Monica Jackson	
Midnight Magic	Gwynne Forster	$8.95
Midnight Peril	Vicki Andrews	$10.95
My Buffalo Soldier	Barbara B. K. Reeves	$8.95
Naked Soul	Gwynne Forster	$8.95
No Regrets	Mildred E. Riley	$8.95
Nowhere to Run	Gay G. Gunn	$10.95
Object of His Desire	A. C. Arthur	$8.95
One Day at a Time	Bella McFarland	$8.95
Passion	T.T. Henderson	$10.95
Past Promises	Jahmel West	$8.95
Path of Fire	T.T. Henderson	$8.95
Picture Perfect	Reon Carter	$8.95

Pride & Joi	Gay G. Gunn	$8.95
Quiet Storm	Donna Hill	$8.95
Reckless Surrender	Rochelle Alers	$8.95
Rendezvous with Fate	Jeanne Sumerix	$8.95
Revelations	Cheris F. Hodges	$8.95
Rivers of the Soul	Leslie Esdaile	$8.95
Rooms of the Heart	Donna Hill	$8.95
Shades of Brown	Denise Becker	$8.95
Shades of Desire	Monica White	$8.95
Sin	Crystal Rhodes	$8.95
So Amazing	Sinclair LeBeau	$8.95
Somebody's Someone	Sinclair LeBeau	$8.95
Someone to Love	Alicia Wiggins	$8.95
Soul to Soul	Donna Hill	$8.95
Still Waters Run Deep	Leslie Esdaile	$8.95
Subtle Secrets	Wanda Y. Thomas	$8.95
Sweet Tomorrows	Kimberly White	$8.95
The Color of Trouble	Dyanne Davis	$8.95
The Price of Love	Sinclair LeBeau	$8.95
The Reluctant Captive	Joyce Jackson	$8.95
The Missing Link	Charlyne Dickerson	$8.95
Three Wishes	Seressia Glass	$8.95
Tomorrow's Promise	Leslie Esdaile	$8.95
Truly Inseperable	Wanda Y. Thomas	$8.95
Twist of Fate	Beverly Clark	$8.95
Unbreak My Heart	Dar Tomlinson	$8.95
Unconditional Love	Alicia Wiggins	$8.95
When Dreams A Float	Dorothy Elizabeth Love	$8.95
Whispers in the Night	Dorothy Elizabeth Love	$8.95
Whispers in the Sand	LaFlorya Gauthier	$10.95
Yesterday is Gone	Beverly Clark	$8.95
Yesterday's Dreams, Tomorrow's Promises	Reon Laudat	$8.95
Your Precious Love	Sinclair LeBeau	$8.95

Subscribe Today
to
Blackboard Times

The African-American
Entertainment Magazine

Get the latest in book reviews, author interviews, book rankings, hottest and
latest TV shows, theater listings and more . . .

Coming in September
blackboardtimes.com

Order Form

Mail to: Genesis Press, Inc.

P.O. Box 101
Columbus, MS 39703

Name _____

Address _____

City/State _____ Zip _____

Telephone _____

Ship to (if different from above)

Name _____

Address _____

City/State _____ Zip _____

Telephone _____

Credit Card Information

Credit Card # _____ ☐ Visa   ☐ Mastercard

Expiration Date (mm/yy) _____ ☐ AmEx   ☐ Discover

Qty.	Author	Title	Price	Total

Use this order form, or call 1-888-INDIGO-1	Total for books _____ Shipping and handling: $5 first two books, $1 each additional book _____ Total S & H _____ Total amount enclosed _____ *Mississippi residents add 7% sales tax*